TILL DEATH DO WE START

Book 4

G.L. Wagner

Thanks to all who supported me through this incredible journey

CHAPTER 1

T ears brimmed in Emily's eyes, spilling over like the first drops of a long-awaited storm. Each one caught the light, tiny prisms against her cheeks. She breathed in deep, the scent of wax and roses enveloping her in the moment.

"Tom," she managed, her voice a tremor, her hand reaching out, fingers trembling as they found his shoulder.

The room spun ever so slightly, a carousel of emotions. She blinked, and for an instant, she saw their lives together— flashes of laughter, of shared moments, of quiet mornings and thunderous nights.

"Yes," she whispers, her voice barely above the rustle of leaves outside. "Yes, Tom Blackwell, I will marry you." A single tear escaping, tracing a path down her cheek, mingling with the joy that already fills her heart.

Cassidy exhales, laughter and tears colliding in a burst of emotion. "Dad, Emily, I'm so happy for both of you!" she exclaimed, rushing to envelop them in an embrace .

"Now this is worth a proper celebration," Tom said smiling. His salt-and-pepper hair catches the dim light, reflecting his newfound vigor. The stoic mask he often wears fades, revealing just a glimpse of the sensitive soul beneath.

"That would be amazing," Emily nods, her green eyes alight. She reaches for Cassidy's hand. "Us and our closest friends."

The phone calls are brief. Within the hour, Jack, Helen, Josh, and Nora converge at the Blackwell's residence, each carrying the weight of their own stories – some visible, like Jack's cropped gray hair, some hidden, like Helen's concealed intelligence behind those thick glasses.

"Congratulations, you two," Jack grumbles, a grin tugging at his lips as he claps Tom on the back. "About time someone made an honest woman out of you, Em."

"Jack!" Helen chides, though her eyes dance with mirth. She offers Emily a warm hug, the jealousy that once gnawed at her fading into genuine happiness for her friend.

Nora arrives with homemade treats, her silver hair shining like a beacon of comfort. "Nothing but the best for this occasion," she declares, spreading out a feast of oysters, lobster, pasta and some salads.

Even young Josh, standing taller both in reality and figuratively now that the shadow of his past are dissipating, manages a broad smile. "This is great news," he says earnestly, though his gaze often drifts toward Cassidy, secretly stealing glances.

Laughter echoes through the Blackwell home, mingling with the clink of glasses filled with Champagne and Pinot grigio, coupled with the soft undertones of Nora's storytelling. It's the sounds of happiness, utter contentment.

"Here's to the start of something new," Tom raises his glass, the words resonating deeper than the clinking crystal.

"Cheers," they echo, each voice adding its unique timbre to the harmony of celebration.

Cassidy leans back in her chair, as a wisp of brown hair falls across her forehead. She brushes it aside, her gaze flitting between the elated couple and Josh. Her father's eyes crinkle at the corners, his smile as wide as the horizon. Emily's hand finds Tom's, their fingers entwining like vines that have finally found their trellis. Cassidy's heart swells as joy bubbles up inside her, a silent laugh waiting to escape.

"Earth to Cassidy," Josh teases, nudging her under the table with his knee. His voice is a lifeline, pulling her back from the sea of emotion threatening to pull her under.

"Sorry," she grins, her eyes meeting his. "Just caught up in all this...ugh, happiness."

"Planning your own fairytale wedding already?" he quips, an eyebrow arching playfully.

"Ha! In your dreams, Harding." But her teasing tone can't mask the blush creeping up her cheeks. She imagines them, just for a second – standing there, in the future, maybe not so different from her dad and Emily.

"Maybe not a wedding," Josh says, leaning closer. "But I can see us... backpacking through Europe? Eating our weight in gelato in Rome?"

"Or getting lost in the catacombs of Paris," Cassidy adds, the words painting pictures of adventure in her mind. "No map, no plan, just us and the city of lights."

"Sounds perfect, I'll start working on my French." He said with a smile. Eyes locked, as if an agreement formed, a pact without words.

"Vraiment," she said with a fake French accent with an east coast under tone, her smile lingering as she turns her attention back to the celebration, the warmth of the moment still tingling in her chest.

They decide to take the celebration outside and all walkout to head to Nora's diner, with the sunlight pouring on them as the spotlight would the actors on a stage. The air carries an easy quietude, only to be broken by the soft clink of cutlery and the muted murmur of conversations once they got to the diner. Dust motes danced in the lazy shafts of light, swirling around diners as if celebrating the day's gentle pace. Nora gets back to work, and Jack walks Helen home.

Outside, across the street Tom and Emily step into the town square, a picture of the glory of late spring. Children dash about, their shrieks of delight punctuating the afternoon while birds add a melodic backdrop, chirping from the branches overhead.

"I love the sound of spring" Emily says, her voice a low hum of contentment, she squeezes Tom's hand.

"Music to my ears," Tom replies, his stoic facade cracking into a smile that reaches his sea-glass eyes. He stops, allowing the tableau of the town to impress upon him – its tranquility, its ordinariness, and yet, at that moment, its sheer perfection.

Tom halts beneath the shade of an old maple, his gaze catching Emily's. A soft breeze plays with her auburn hair as he reaches behind the gnarled trunk, his hand emerging with a bouquet of wildflowers, their colors vivid against the green backdrop.

"Emily," he says, offering them to her, "for you," as he bowed in a comically exaggerated form.

Her eyes soften, the green there deepening as she takes in the simple beauty of the daisies, poppies, and bluebells. She leans in, inhaling the earthy fragrance, a natural perfume that speaks of open fields and new beginnings.

"Tom, they're beautiful," she breathes out, with a slight giggle at his fake gallantry.

Nearby, Cassidy laughs, the sound carrying on the wind. She emerges from around a bend in the path, Josh in tow, his own smile a mirror of her joy. They approach, the park enveloping them all in its leafy embrace.

"Look at you two," Cassidy teases, "the picture of romance."

"Careful, Cass," Josh chimes in, nudging her playfully, "you might get the disease too."

She sticks out her tongue, but her eyes dance with undeniable emotion. Tom watches them, this is their future unfolding— bright, hopeful.

"Shall we?" Emily gestures down the path, her arm looping through Tom's once more.

They walk together, the foliage brisling happy thoughts above them. The sun filters through the leaves, dappling the ground with patches of light and shadow.

"Remember when we used to race up this hill?" Cassidy asks Josh, pointing towards a gentle slope crowned with dandelions.

"Only because you'd cheat and start early every time, like e-v-e-r-y time" he retorts, but his grin betrays his mock indignation.

Tom laughs, the sound mingling with the birdcalls overhead. Emily squeezes his arm, her gesture weaving her affection into the very air around them. It's a moment suspended in time, a memory already etched into their brains.

"Ready, go!" Cassidy's voice cuts through the stillness, playful challenge lighting her eyes. She springs forward, a laugh spilling from her lips as her feet slap against the cobblestones. Josh reacts with a slow start, but he's quick to chase after her, catching up with long strides that eat up the ground between them.

"Cheater, again" he accuses lightly, reaching out to playfully tug at her sleeve. But Cassidy darts away, her wavy brown hair streaming behind her like a banner of rebellion.

"Got to be faster than that!" she calls over her shoulder, her laughter echoing off the quaint buildings lining their path.

Tom and Emily pause, sharing an amused glance before their gazes follow the two figures racing ahead. The sight of Cassidy and Josh, so carefree and full of life, stirs something warm in Tom's chest, a gentle swell of pride and affection that Emily senses without a word being spoken.

"Those two," Emily murmurs, her eyes sparkling with fondness.

"Reminds me of us when we were young," Tom replies, his smile genuine and unguarded.

"Speaking of youth," Tom says after a beat, the idea surfacing like a bubble of nostalgia, "how about we hit the local ice cream shop? It's been a while since we've indulged, like at least an hour."

"Sounds perfect," Emily agrees, her grin spreading wide. "You know I can't resist their brownie scattered vanilla."

As Tom and Emily catch up to the two would be racers, Tom but has the time to mutter- "Ice Cream?"- before the eyes of both

Cassidy and Josh glimmer with agreement.

"Race you there!" Cassidy shouts back at them.

"Come on, old folks!" Cassidy teases, beckoning to Tom and Emily with a mischievous twinkle in her blue eyes. "Do you need a head start^"

"Old, huh?" Tom chuckles, accepting the challenge. He takes Emily's hand in his, and they set off at a leisurely pace, content to let the youngsters revel in their mock victory.

"First one to pick their flavor gets to pick the movie tonight!" Cassidy calls over her shoulder, her laughter cascading through the air like a melody.

"Deal! But prepare for a double feature of classic westerns," Tom shouts back, his competitive edge peeking through despite the lighthearted atmosphere.

"Only if you can catch us!" Josh teases, and with a shared look, he and Cassidy sprint ahead, their youthful energy propelling them forward. Tom watches them go, a contented sigh escaping him. He squeezes Emily's hand tighter, and she looks up at him, her eyes shining with love and a hint of playful challenge.

"Shall we?" she asks, and together, they quicken their pace, not to win but to join in the joyous celebration of the moment.

Their footsteps hit the cobblestone with the distant chimes of laughter from Cassidy and Josh ahead. The late afternoon sun dips lower, casting long shadows that dance around them, weaving through the serene tableau of the town.

"Life is good, isn't it?" Emily says, her voice soft yet brimming with happiness.

"Better than I ever imagined," Tom agrees, and as they approach the ice cream shop, the smell of sweet cream and sugar greets them, wrapping around the group like a promise of simple pleasures and shared memories.

"Make way for the champions!" Cassidy exclaims, reaching the door first, her arm looped through Josh's as they hold it open for Tom and Emily.

"Thank you, kind sirs," Emily says with a laugh, stepping through the threshold into the cool embrace of the shop, where a new chapter of their lives waits to be written, one scoop at a time.

The bell above the door chimes as Tom, Emily, Cassidy, and Josh step into the ice cream shop. The rich scent of vanilla, chocolate and baking waffle cones fills the air, and a collective smile spreads across their faces. Tom glances at the array of flavors, each vibrant color calling out for attention, while Emily leans closer to the glass, her eyes reflecting the swirls of mint chocolate chip.

"Strawberry cheesecake, please," Cassidy declares, her voice bubbling with excitement. She turns to Josh, raising an eyebrow in challenge. "Can you handle the triple chocolate fudge, or is it too much for you?"

Josh grins back, undaunted. "Only if you're ready to admit that my choice tops yours."

Behind them, Tom opts for his usual—butter pecan. A nod of approval from the scooper meets his decision. Emily hesitates, caught between her brownie supreme and pistachio, before settling on the latter with a satisfied nod.

They take their treasures outside, where the late afternoon sun still offers its warmth. Seated around a wrought-iron table, they unwrap napkins from plastic spoons and dive in. Laughter spills forth as Josh recounts how Cassidy almost tripped during their impromptu race, and she swats his arm playfully, her cheeks rosy with mirth.

"Hey, I let you win," she protests, but her eyes dance with shared humor.

"Sure you did," Josh chuckles, licking a stubborn drip of chocolate from his cone.

Tom watches them, his heart swelling with a father's pride. He catches Emily's eye, as they share this moment of contentment. As the laughter continues, stories flow like the river nearby— a mix of past adventures and future dreams. Ice cream melts, sweet and slow, a perfect metaphor for the ease of this day.

Tom sets his spoon down, the metal clinking against the porcelain of the bowl. A breeze whispers through the leaves overhead, carrying with it the laughter of children from the nearby park. He turns to Emily, her green eyes reflecting the softening light. "Emily," he begins, his voice steady but imbued with emotion, "I can't believe how much has changed. How much we've... healed since finding each other."

Emily's lips curve in a gentle smile; she reaches across the table, her fingers brushing his. "Life's funny like that," she muses aloud. "Just when you think all the chapters have ended, a new story begins." The words hang between them, simple yet profound.

"Indeed," Tom agrees, feeling the weight of years of loneliness lifting off his shoulders. "I've spent so long building walls, never realizing that what I needed was someone who'd walk through them without hesitation."

"Tom," she interjects softly, "you gave me trust when I had none left for myself. You showed me that love isn't a fortress to hide behind, but a bridge to cross together."

They sit in silence for a moment, letting the truth of their words settle over them like the evening's first stars twinkling to life above.

At a nearby table, Cassidy sneaks a glance at Josh. Their knees touch accidentally under the table, sending a current of awareness through them both. They look away quickly, then back again, Josh's hand moves beneath the table, fingers tentatively seeking hers. Her hand meets his, a secret clasp that says more than words could.

Their connection is a fragile thing, made of confidences in times of trouble and knowing looks, but in it lies the strength of trust. Cassidy wonders about the future, about stepping out of her father's shadow and into a light of her own making—with Josh by her side.

"Hey," Josh murmurs, drawing her out of her reverie, "you know we're gonna need to start looking into universities, right?"

Cassidy's heart skips. She nods, a rush of affection flooding her senses. "Yeah, we will."

Around them, the golden hour fades to dusk, its tranquility wrapping around the group like a warm shawl. There are no grand gestures or proclamations—just the quiet understanding that they have found solace in one another amidst the chaos of life.

The sun dips lower, casting a soft orange glow on the faces of the group as they rise from their seats outside the ice cream shop. Laughter ebbs and flows with the ease of long-standing friendships.

"Best decision I ever made," Tom says, his voice a gentle rumble, eyes not leaving Emily's as he grabbed her hand in both his.

"Seconded," Emily replies, her gaze locked with his, a smile playing on her lips that reaches her green eyes.

Cassidy pushes back her chair, standing beside Josh. Their shoulders barely brush, an electric charge passing between them. She watches her father and Emily, her heart swelling in her chest. This is a new chapter, not just for Tom, but for all of them.

"Shall we?" Tom's voice cuts through the moment, easy and teasing as he gestures towards the parking lot. Emily chuckles, shaking her head at his impatience, but there's a softness in her gaze as she looks at him.

"Race you to the cars?" Cassidy challenges, a spark of mischief lighting up her blue eyes.

"I'm getting to old for this" Tom said in a halfhearted fakish kind of way.

Josh grins, accepting the playful dare. They take off, their footsteps light against the cobblestone path, laughter trailing behind them. For a moment, they're not burdened by the past or worries of the future—they are simply young and alive, racing toward whatever comes next.

Tom and Emily walk more slowly, savoring the simple joy of being together. The air carries the scent of blooming flowers and the fading warmth of the day. A bird's song punctuates the calm, melding with distant sounds of children still at play.

"Life's full of surprises, huh?" Emily muses aloud.

"Only the best kind," Tom assures her, squeezing her hand, sending a silent vow through their touch.

Behind them, Nora steps out of the diner, her silver hair catching the last rays of sunlight. She observes the group fondly, knowing glances exchanged with each goodbye. Contentment settles in her chest; this is the fabric of the community she loves.

As they reach their cars, the group pauses, not ready to say goodbye. They stand in a circle, each one taking a moment to look around at their friends and the town they call home. In this moment, they feel a deep sense of gratitude for the bond they share and the memories they've created.

"Take care of my girl, Tom," Cassidy calls out, half-joking, half-serious, as she slides into the passenger seat of Josh's car.

"Always have, always will," Tom replies, meeting his daughter's gaze with a promise.

The cars pull away, leaving behind an empty town square. The street lamps flicker on, casting pools of light onto empty benches and quiet storefronts. But the absence of the group leaves a palpable space that will soon be filled again with their stories, their laughter, and their love for each other.

CHAPTER 2

Sunlight spills across the oak tabletop, a gentle warmth that dances over the steaming mugs between Tom and Emily. In his kitchen, a haven of soft shadows and quietude, they huddle close, lost in shared laughter. Tom's eyes, flecked with the wisdom of his years, crinkle at the corners as he brushes a stray lock from Emily's face. His touch is tender, his smile genuine—a reflection of a heart mending its fractures.

Emily's gaze rests on him, her green eyes reflecting an unspoken depth. She leans into his caress, allowing herself this moment of reprieve. The silence envelops them, a comforting embrace that whispers of new beginnings and healed scars.

But peace is a fickle guest. The shrill ring of a phone slices through the calm, a discordant note in their morning symphony. Emily's hand halts midair, the laughter fading from her lips. She casts a glance at the hellish device before picking up.

"Hello?" Her voice, once light with mirth, hardens. The transformation is subtle yet swift; her posture straightens, her free hand clenches into a fist. Tom watches the change, his lawyer's mind already cataloging details—the pitch of her tone, the tightening of her jaw.

As she listens, her expression shifts—shadows pass over her features like clouds over a stormy sea. The muscles in Tom's neck tense, anticipating, preparing. Something has breached their sanctuary, something grim.

"Understood," Emily says, a finality in her voice that chills the room. She places the phone down with a precision that betrays her control slipping. Silence claims the space again, yet now it hums with urgency, a prelude to the tempest that awaits them beyond these walls.

Tom leans forward, the scrape of his chair against the tile floor a harsh echo in the charged air. His eyes, sharp and assessing, drinking in every nuance of Emily's face—each line of tension, each subtle shift betraying her inner turmoil.

"Emily?" His voice is a low thrum of concern, the name slipping from him as both question and anchor.

She ends the call with a decisive click, a signal that their quiet morning is now a relic of the past. Her gaze meets his, the green of her eyes darkening with the gravity of what she's about to disclose. "There's been a murder," she says, the words heavy, urgent. "At one of the foster homes."

Disbelief widens Tom's eyes, a flicker of shock before his features harden into resolve. Emily's fingers find the familiar weight of her badge, the cool metal grounding her as reality surges forth. The lawyer in Tom battles with the fiancé; questions claw at his mind, demanding attention, but he suppresses them—for her.

"Details?" he asks, despite himself, the lawyer's instinct too strong to ignore.

"Later," she answers, curt, the sheriff now eclipsing the woman who had basked in the tranquility of the morning only moments ago.

They stand together, the room suddenly too small, the day ahead too vast. Emily's hand on her badge is a silent vow—a promise to seek justice, to chase the truth wherever it may lead. And though Tom knows he should step back, let her do her job, the pull to protect, to solve, to understand, is a tide he can barely resist.

Tom snatches his jacket from the back of a chair, keys jingling as he scoops them from the counter. Emily, badge in hand, mirrors him, her movements swift, the crisp snap of her leather jacket a sharp punctuation to the urgency that has gripped them both.

Their eyes lock for a heartbeat, a silent exchange passing between them. His gaze is steel wrapped in velvet concern; hers, a blaze of professional resolve.

They burst through the door, feet pounding the wooden porch steps. The world outside greets them with an eerie hush, the quietness of Oakwood's streets contrasting sharply with the rush of adrenaline that fuels their stride. The town seems paused, as if the news of calamity hangs heavy in the air, yet to ripple through the community's consciousness.

Their pace quickens, shoes striking pavement in tandem, the early morning chill bites at their faces, their minds already racing towards the chaos that awaits at the station.

"Feels like the calm before the storm," Tom mutters, breath forming clouds in the cool air.

"Let's hope we're the thunder," Emily replies, her voice laced with a tenacity that would make the looming clouds envious.

As they near the station, the stillness of Oakwood seems to press in around them, a stark contrast to the flurry of motion within their chests. With each step closer, the weight of the day's responsibilities settles heavier on their shoulders, a mantle they bear without question.

They reach the entrance, the glass doors reflecting back their determined silhouettes. Without hesitation, they push through, ready to confront the tempest that brews inside.

The station's atmosphere crackles with urgency, a hive of officers in motion, their faces drawn tight with gravity. Emily strides into the fray, a conductor amidst dissonance, her voice ringing clear and authoritative. "Davis, get the M.E. on the line. Harris, I need eyes on the street cams." Deputies scatter, spurred into action by her commands.

Beside her, Tom hovers at the periphery, an island in the stream of activity. His gaze sharpens, a keen edge to his scrutiny as he absorbs the details: furrowed brows, hushed conversations, fingers dancing over keyboards. His hand reaches for a notepad, the familiar weight grounding him. Pen in hand, he scribbles, lines and words corralling the tumult into order.

"Tom, you don't have to do this," Emily's voice slices through his focus, green eyes locking onto his.

A shrug lifts his shoulders, nonchalant yet deliberate. "Old habits," he offers, the corner of his mouth quirking up, a flash of levity amid the storm.

He turns back to observe, noting the comings and goings, the fragments of dialogue that float his way. Patterns emerge, a narrative assembling itself from disjointed pieces. He is peripheral, yet central; an observer, yet undeniably part of the unfolding drama.

Emily moves with precision, her commands sculpting the chaos into something resembling progress. She's the epicenter of the investigation, each officer an extension of her will.

Tom watches, admiration laced with concern etching his features. The ruffled lawyer knows his place is not within these walls, but he can't help but engage, his mind weaving through the labyrinth of facts and speculation. Dry wit meets earnest concern within him, a balance that keeps him at peace yet alert.

Emily stands in the eye of the storm, her voice commanding as she dispatches officers with the urgency of a general at war. Her auburn hair flares like a banner in the frenetic light of the station, each officer's hurried steps a beat in the symphony she conducts.

"Check Morgan's phone records," she instructs, "And someone canvass the neighborhood again. We need more than we've got."

Jack strides up, his stocky frame cutting through the buzz. "Time of death's between 12 and 2 AM. hard to tell yet with the window busted open. Neighbors heard nothing." His gruff voice bears the weight of unwelcome news, yet Emily nods, assimilating the detail into her mental map of the crime.

"Shot, close range," he continues, "Silencer, maybe?"

"Likely," she confirms. Her green eyes narrow, calculating. "Gather everything on her ex—Jonathan Reynolds. He's out of town, but I want his alibi watertight."

Tom leans against a cold wall, scribbling in his notepad, the lines on his face deepening with thought. A lawyer lost in a sea of detectives, his presence is an anomaly; his mind, however, is right at home amongst the tangled threads of evidence. He sketches the outline of facts, the profile of a murder half-glimpsed in shadows.

The air crackles with tension, the officers' collective breaths painting an invisible fog of determination and frustration. Tom catches Emily's gaze for a fleeting moment—their silent exchange, a mutual recognition of the stakes at hand. She turns away, diving back into the fray, leaving Tom to wrestle with the gravity of their unspoken pact.

"Her foster kids," Tom murmurs, almost to himself, "Clara and Charles... what do they know?" His question hangs, unanswered, amidst the clatter of keyboards and the shuffle of papers.

"Dead ends everywhere," an officer mutters, passing by.

"Dead ends are just detours," Emily counters without missing a step, her retort sharp as a blade. "Find me something I can use."

Tom's lips curve, a wry smile that doesn't reach his eyes. His gaze lingers on her, pride and concern warring in the depths of his expression. The ruffled lawyer, tethered to the tempestuous sheriff by more than just a case—a shared quest for justice amidst the chaos of Oakwood's darkest hour.

Hours tick by in a blur of activity, the officers tirelessly combing through evidence and following leads. Tom's mind is racing, piecing together the facts like an intricate puzzle. He watches as Emily moves with razor-sharp focus, her eyes scanning the room for any new developments.

The walls of the station seem to close in on them, the air heavy with anticipation. Tom can feel the tension building, the weight of the investigation bearing down on them all. But he can also sense the determination in the room, the shared goal of bringing justice to Morgan Reynolds.

As the sun begins to set, Emily gathers her team for a quick meeting. Tom watches from the sidelines, his lawyer instincts kicking in as he takes notes and tries to make sense of the chaos.

"Time of death was around midnight," Emily says, her voice sharp and focused. "We've narrowed down the list of suspects to those who had access to the foster home that night. Including Clara and Charles Leblanc."

Tom's eyebrows shoot up at the mention of the children. He had noticed their absence earlier, but hadn't considered them as possible suspects. He scribbles their names down in his notepad, his mind already spinning with new possibilities.

"Let's keep digging," Emily continues, her tone unwavering. "We're getting closer, I can feel it."

Tom nods along, his mind racing with theories and ideas. The investigation is far from over, but he knows they're making progress. And with Emily leading the charge, he has no doubt that justice will be served.

Their footsteps echo off the station's floor as Tom and Emily stride through the double doors. The day's grueling work has set a spark in Emily's eyes; she's a woman on a mission, her thoughts churning with leads and evidence. Beside her, Tom wrestles with an urge to dive into the fray, his lawyer's mind teeming with questions and connections. But he quashes it down; this is police business, and Emily and Jack are more than capable.

The evening air nips at their skin, a refreshing contrast to the stagnant warmth of the office they've left behind. Oakwood stirs around them, its slumbering streets waking up as twilight unfurls across the sky. Shop fronts hum to life, neon signs buzzing like fireflies caught in jars, casting pools of light that dance on the pavement. It's ordinary town life, but tonight, it feels like a scene from some hopeful narrative where darkness doesn't last forever.

Emily's breath forms clouds in the chilly air, her green eyes reflecting the town lights like twin beacons cutting through the night. She pulls her jacket tighter, the badge pinned to her chest catching a stray beam and winking brightly. Tom stands by, his own breath mingling with hers, watching the usual bustle with an uncommon attention. He notices things—the way the streetlights flicker before steadying, the shift of shadows as people pass, each one a potential chapter in their investigation's unfolding story.

"Think you're onto something?" Tom asks, his voice low and steady, betraying none of the storm of thoughts inside him.

"Feels like it," Emily responds, her tone mirroring his, though the undercurrent of urgency is unmistakable. "Just need that break, you know? We'll get some questioning done, but I know we will find the person."

They pause at the curb, cars whispering past, their headlights slicing through the gathering dusk. There's no reply needed; they both understand the game too well. Breaks either come or they don't, and sometimes all the grinding determination in the world can't force the pieces to fit.

"Let's grab some dinner," Tom suggests, attempting to shift gears from the intensity of the investigation. "You've got to eat."

"Can't," Emily replies curtly, her eyes reflecting the resolve that has become her armor. "I have to check on Clara and Charles tonight."

"Alright," he concedes, respecting her dedication. He watches her stride away, then turns his gaze to the town.

CHAPTER 3

Clara Leblanc perches on the edge of a cushioned chair, her spine a rigid line of tension. The waiting room's clock ticks in rhythm with her jittery foot, each second stretching like taffy. She wraps her arms around herself, trying to ward off the chill that doesn't come from the room's temperature.

Tom Blackwell strides through the front door, a greeting for each face he passes. His salt-and-pepper hair seems more pepper than salt today, his posture straighter, as if Emily's acceptance of his proposal has infused him with vigor. He brushes past the potted plants, sparing them only a cursory glance before vanishing into the sanctuary of his office.

Helen Sedlak observes from behind thick lenses, noting Tom's mood. A flicker of something – a mix of old affection and new resignation – crosses her features before she smooths them back into professional lines. Her heels click a determined beat against the linoleum as she approaches Tom's door.

"Tom," she starts, leaning against the jamb with poise, "that girl, Clara Leblanc? She's been waiting since dawn cracked. Says it's urgent."

"Persistent, is she?" Tom's words float from behind the mahogany desk, his tone more curious than concerned.

"Like a winter's chill." Helen hesitates, adjusting her glasses. "She's small but there's an intensity to her... hard to ignore."

"Alright, send her in." Tom leans back, fingers tented, eyes already dissecting this new puzzle named Clara Leblanc.

The door swings open, silent on well-oiled hinges. Clara Leblanc steps over the threshold, her movements betraying nothing of the turmoil within. She's a glacier in a dress, poised and chillingly serene while also having braded pig tails. Tom observes from behind his desk, noting the subtle tremors that quake through her small hands – the only thing leaking the fear lurking in the depths of her wide, haunted eyes.

"Clara," he begins, voice even, a rock amidst the swirling uncertainty. "Please, take a seat."

She complies, folding into the offered chair like a shadow seeking solace from the sun. Her gaze fixes to his, like a plea transmitted in the flicker of her eyelids.

"Mr. Blackwell," her voice is a whisper of winter wind, carrying flakes of dread. "I'm not sure where else to turn. They say my brother and I... they say we're killers. But it's a lie."

"I see," Tom prompts, the edge of his curiosity transcending.

"Charlie and I, we're been framed for something monstrous, something we couldn't conceive in our most troubled dreams." Clara's articulation belies her youth, each word a carefully spoken. "The foster home, it was supposed to be a home, but now it's a theater where this macabre play unfolds and we are unwilling actors thrust upon the stage."

Tom's fingers tap an absent rhythm on mahogany, interested, but also surprised at the theatrical expressions coming from this kid, who can't be older then twelve. The room feels colder, as if her words summon the chill of doubt and suspicion.

"Your reputation precedes you," she continues, eyes never straying. "You find the truth hidden beneath deceit. That's why I'm here. You're my brother and I's final hope, my last ember in a night that threatens to swallow us whole."

He nods, the gesture slow, deliberate. "You have my attention, Clara, but answer this first, where in gods name did you learn to speak like that?"

A small smile creeped across her face, taking this as a compliment, "You see Mr Blackwell, as a foster child, I have never had much, but the only things i do have from my parents are some books, my father was a Classics professor and my mother and English lit student."

"Oh, I see, well I'm sorry for your loss Clara, I won't lie it's true you're a suspect, but it's also true your case does have intrigue. After meeting you I do want to know more, so I might take your case, but I warn you no lies, or else I won't be able to help."

Her relief is palpable, a thawing in the frost that clads her heart. But the air remains tense, charged with the weight of a case that will demand every ounce of Tom's resolve.

Tom settles behind his desk, the leather chair creaking under the shift of his weight. He steeples his fingers, eyes locked on Clara's pale face as she perches on the edge of the visitor's seat across from him. The silence hangs heavy between them, laden with anticipation and the unspoken gravity of the situation.

"Begin at the start," Tom says, voice firm but not unkind. "Spare no detail."

Clara inhales, her chest rising sharply beneath her thin sweater. "It began with an argument, before bed" she starts, voice steady despite the tremor Tom notices in her hands. "Mrs. Reynolds, the caretaker, accused Charles of stealing—a trinket of no real value. But he didn't take it."

"Ok," Tom muses aloud, recalling the police's assertion of theft as a motive. "And this disagreement, did it escalate?"

"We're kids, Mr. Blackwell, so yes of course it escalated, but nothing unusual, Charles got yelled at, he doesn't like being accused even if he's done something wrong." Clara's gaze drops to her lap. "But we retreated to our room, for our punishment, no other thoughts."

"Yet someone acted on such thoughts," Tom interjects. His mind races, piecing together the mismatched fragments of information.

"Later that night, a scream pierced the silence," Clara whispers. "We found her... Mrs. Reynolds, lifeless on the kitchen floor."

"Did anyone else see you there? Before the discovery?" Tom leans forward, instincts honed like a blade ready to slice through obfuscation.

"Only Emma, another foster child." Clara's brow furrows, a new wrinkle of worry. "She wouldn't speak against us, I'm certain."

"Odd," Tom murmurs to himself, recalling no mention of Emma from last night's briefing. "Go on."

"Charles tried to help, he saw CPR on TV once, so he tried to revive her, but..." She trails off, swallowing hard against the memory.

"His prints would be on her, then," Tom deduces, filing away each revelation. "Convenient for constructing guilt."

"Exactly," Clara nods, relief mingling with desperation in her eyes. "But he was only trying to bring her back."

"Indeed," Tom acknowledges, his belief in the child cementing. He rises, a thought taking shape in his movement. "Well, Miss Leblanc, we have much to do."

Her sigh is a soft exhalation of fears momentarily eased. Tom, already plotting his next move, feels the familiar thrill of the chase awakening. The game is afoot.

Tom stands, a sentinel against the encroaching shadows of doubt and accusation. The air in his office seems charged, heavy with Clara's silent plea. He nods, once, decisively. "Clara, you and Charles will have your day, I'll take your case."

Relief blooms on her face, a rare flower in winter's grip. She nods, a mirror to his resolve.

"So First, we have to talk to Charles," Tom says. His fingers drumming a beat on the oak desk — the beat of justice pacing through his veins. "Where is your brother Clara?"

"The police brought us to orphanage last night, he's still there." Clara stated mater-of-factly.

"Let's go talk to your little brother then, shall we?"

Tom and Clara go out to talk to her little brother. He is extremely intrigued by this young girl, half adult half child, thinking about the pain of growing up with no real family, he really hoped he could help. They find Charles in the visitation room, a place of sterile walls and watchful eyes. The boy's energy is caged, his humor dark. Yet, when he sees Clara, a spark ignites, fleeting but fierce.

"Hello Charles," Tom begins, voice even, "I'd like to talk to you about that night."

As if waiting for his sisters cue, Charles looks to Clara who nods in agreement, letting him know it's safe to talk.

A tide of words spills from Charles, details lapping over each other, eager to be heard. Tom listens, sifting truth from youthful exuberance. He repeats the same story his sister had told Tom no more then an hour ago.

"Emma can back us up," Charles insists, his confidence unflagging.

"Good. We'll need her corroboration," Tom replies, mind mapping out the labyrinthine turnings of the investigation ahead. His gaze meets Clara's; this is but the first step.

"Anyone else come and go that evening?" Tom probes, eyes never straying from Charles' animated face.

"Mr. Hobb was there, fixing a leak," Charles blurts, then clamps his mouth shut as though he's said too much.

"Interesting," Tom mulls over the new lead.

"Alright. You've both been very very brave," Tom commends. The children's spirits lift minutely, buoyed by belief in their new advocate.

Outside the room, Tom's strides are purposeful. Every interview, every question draws him deeper into the tangle of events surrounding the murder.

"Next, we speak to Emma," he tells Clara, already anticipating the hurdles ahead.

"Then Mr. Hobb," she adds quietly, her intellect sharp as a blade.

"Right." Tom's reply is quizzical, caught of guard by Clara's understanding of the situation, his dry wit is sheathed for now.

Tom Blackwell's hands shuffle through the scatter of documents, his fingers tracing the fine print of crime scene reports and forensic results. He pauses, absorbing every detail, every inconsistency. The office around him is still, save for the whir of a ceiling fan above.

The door clicks open; Sheriff Emily Foster leans against the frame, her silhouette haloed by the light from the corridor. "Working late? I thought you were helping me out with this one," she says, the words tinged with an expectation of camaraderie.

"Helping out? Well no you said I should stay out" Tom looks up, meets her gaze—a mixture of forest green and challenge. "And good thing too, these are my new clients, Emily. Clara and Charles Leblanc."

Her eyes widen slightly, then narrow, a ripple of confusion and annoyance passing over her features. "Clara and Charles? Why on Earth would you—"

"Because I believe them to be innocent, first thing this morning I came in, Clara was waiting for me, we talked, I believed her ." His voice is firm, resolute as bedrock. "And they need someone to believe them."

Emily steps inside, closing the door behind her with a soft click. She crosses her arms, skeptical. "Innocent? They're suspects, Tom. You know what everyone's saying."

"Since when do we take 'everyone's saying' for gospel?" he counters, his tone edged with that dry wit of his. "I'm following leads, visiting the foster home, speaking to neighbors. There's history there, Emily. Motives, the truth."

She watches him, the irk in her stance softening into contemplation. "You really think there's more to it?"

"Always is, isn't there?" He taps the stack of papers. "Wouldn't hurt to look beyond the surface, would it?"

"Are you just doing this because I told you to stay out of this one?" Her question comes grudgingly, but it's there, hanging between them.

"Wow, have i ever been petty like that before?" Tom stands, stretching stiff muscles. "You should know me better then that, anyhow, tomorrow, I start digging."

"Be careful, Tom." Emily's warning is soft, almost hesitant. "You don't know what could be unturned."

"Careful's my middle name," he quips, but his eyes are serious. "Don't worry about me."

But she does. It's written in the lines of her body as she turns to leave, in the final glance she throws over her shoulder. Tom watches her go, then turns back to his fortress of paperwork, his mind already racing ahead to the next day's quest for answers.

Sunlight breaks through the office blinds, casting long shadows across the clutter on Tom's desk. He sifts through crime scene photos, his fingers stained with printer ink and his mind churning with contradictions. Something doesn't align, and it gnaws at him.

"Twelve-year-old girls don't just turn killers overnight," he mutters to himself, scrutinizing a timeline of events that Clara had sketched out for him. Charles, the energetic boy with a quick smile, hardly fits the profile either.

A witness statement catches his eye – a neighbor claiming to have seen a shadowy figure lurking near the foster home on the night of the murder. No mention of children. Tom leans in, pores tightening around the new lead. The figure's build is too broad, too tall to match either sibling.

"Could be anyone," he whispers, tracing the timeline further back. There's a pattern of break-ins in the area, none of which linked to the siblings. Tom's brow furrows; the authorities had been too quick to pin blame without looking deeper.

He rises from his chair, stretching cramped muscles as he paces the length of the room. His footsteps are soft on the carpet, the only sound in the otherwise silent office. With each step, he pieces together a narrative far removed from the one painted by the police.

"Let's see what the neighbors have been keeping quiet about," he resolves, grabbing his coat. As he steps out into the crisp air, the town seems different to him – not the cozy enclave he grew up in, but a puzzle with pieces askew.

The foster home looms ahead, its walls holding secrets. Tom knocks on doors, listens to the guarded voices sharing hushed stories. A man mentions a heated argument he overheard days before the murder – not involving Clara or Charles. Another clue, another inconsistency.

"Everyone has something to hide," Tom contemplates, his gut telling him the truth lies buried beneath layers of deceit. Each revelation builds momentum, propelling him closer to the obscured heart of the matter.

"Someone's not playing straight," he concludes, determination hardening in his chest. He knows he's onto something, and he won't rest until justice sheds its light on the shadows of this case.

Tom strides into the precinct, his shadow stretching long and lean across the polished floor. The buzz of activity here is a stark contrast to the silence of his office. Officers dart past, their faces etched with the day's burdens. He senses their scrutiny, feels the weight of their collective skepticism.

"Blackwell," barks Sergeant Jack Turner, emerging from the throng like a battleship cutting through calm waters. His gray hair seems to bristle with animosity. "Stirring the pot again?"

"Only when I'm cooking my famous spaghetti sauce," Tom

retorts, a wry twist to his lips as he holds Jack's gaze.

"Clara and Charles," Jack begins, folding thick arms across his chest, "are the DA's prime suspects, they literally had blood on their hands. Why are you muddying the waters?"

"Maybe because the waters were never clear, Jack." Tom's voice is firm, eyes steady.

Emily approaches, her presence commanding the space around them. Her green eyes, usually warm for him, now flash with an intensity that could cut glass. "Tom," she says, her voice laced with a blend of respect and reproof, "why are you doing this?"

"Because it's right," he replies, meeting her gaze head-on, his resolve unflinching. "I've found inconsistencies."

"Which doesn't mean they're innocent," she counters.

"Or guilty," he adds softly, undeterred by her stance. "Anyways, I just wanted to see if you where free for lunch Em."

"I see, well we're kinda busy as you can see, rain check?" Emily stated.

Tom nods and brushes past them, his gait measured, and steps out into the glaring sunlight as he decides to keep on digging.

At the foster home, he surveys the scene. Fingers probe the air, his mind works, sifting through facts and whispers like a gold panner seeking the glint of truth in a river of lies.

"Obstacles be damned," he mutters. The Leblancs' innocence is a beacon, and he'll navigate this stormy sea of doubt with the compass of his conviction.

"Let's see who profits from this," Tom muses, his instincts razor-sharp as he heads to the next lead. As Tom goes through the crime scene, nothing jumps out at him, but he keeps wondering, where would two kids find a gun with a silencer, it made no sense.

"I get that the kids had opportunity as they where here in the middle of the night, but would they have the means to do it? What is there motive? I just don't see it happening." Tom mused as he left the home with more questions then answers.

CHAPTER 4

Tom Blackwell's gray-blue eyes scan the horizon as he leaves the crime scene, a tumult of thoughts churning in his mind. Each clue seems to edge him further from the truth rather than closer. With furrowed brows and hands shoved deep into his pockets, he strides toward the familiar refuge that is Nora's Diner.

The door swings open with a jingle, admitting Tom to the coffee shop's embrace. The din of chatter swells around him; it's a symphony of Oakwood's daily life. Steam curls from mugs like ethereal tendrils, carrying the rich scent of coffee that battles the sea's brine for dominance in the air.

Behind the counter, Nora presides over her domain, a conductor orchestrating the flow of food and conversation. Red vinyl seats cradle their regulars, while the jukebox hums a low, forgotten melody.

"Lost or just wandering?" Nora calls out, a twinkle in her eye betraying the jest in her greeting. It's her way—dry humor wrapped in warm concern.

Tom strides across the checkered floor, his steps sure and swift.

He navigates through the thrum of life in Nora's Diner with a familiarity honed by countless visits. At the counter, the silver-haired proprietor wipes her hands on an apron as she spots him. Their eyes lock—a silent exchange laden with years of camaraderie.

"Tom," Nora greets, her voice a warm lilt over the clatter of dishes. "What brings you in? Coffee, or a mystery to unravel?"

"Both," he admits, easing onto a stool. The counter is polished to a shine, reflecting the worry lines etched into his rugged face. "It's Sarah Reynolds this time. Dead. And I'm grasping at straws trying to figure out why."

Nora's hospitality seems to pause, just for a beat, as the gravity of his words sinks in. She pours him a mug of coffee, the liquid black and promising.

"Talk to me," she urges, sliding the steaming cup across to him.

Tom wraps his hands around the ceramic warmth, the scent of roasted beans grounding him. "Sarah was found at the edge of town, no clear motive. It's like she stumbled into a bad chapter of someone else's story." His thumb traces the rim of the mug. "I need to find the 'why' behind it all. Without that, we're chasing shadows."

"Shadows have a nasty habit of evaporating in the light of day," Nora muses, leaning forward, her gaze steady. "Let's shed some light then, shall we?"

Nora leans in, elbows on the counter, a human anchor in the sea of din and clinking ceramic. Her eyes, sharp as tacks under silver wisps of hair, never stray from Tom's face. She absorbs each detail, sifting fact from Tom's frustration like chaff from wheat.

"Sarah was not one to make enemies," she starts, her words deliberate, pacing the undercurrent of her thoughts. "Her heart was here, with the town and its people."

Tom nods, sipping coffee, waiting for the pearls of her insight to string together.

"Could be someone outside Oakwood, then," Nora posits, tapping a finger against her chin. "A stranger passing through, an old grudge resurfacing?"

"Or something closer." Tom's voice drops to a murmur. "Local secrets have long shadows."

"Indeed." Nora's lips press into a line, thin as the edge of a knife. "And Sarah had a way of stepping into light, didn't she? Perhaps she saw something, something meant to stay hidden."

"An unwitting witness to someone else's sin?" Tom muses aloud, catching her drift.

"Exactly." Nora's gaze flicks to the window, to the streets where secrets dress up as mundane. "Someone with much to lose might panic, turn violent..."

"Desperation breeds recklessness," Tom agrees, his mind racing along the thread she spins. "We need to look at what's changed in Oakwood, who's been acting out of sorts."

"Start with the docks," Nora suggests. "Tides bring in more than fish, and gossip flows freely with the ale."

"Always the pulse of Oakwood," Tom concedes, grateful for her guidance. "Nora, you're a lighthouse in foggy waters."

"Flattery will get you another cup of coffee, councilor," she quips, her smile brief but bright as she refills his mug. "But remember, even lighthouses can't stop every boat from crashing in the deep."

Tom's shoulders unclench as he sips the coffee Nora poured, its warmth seeping into his veins like an old friend's embrace. Her insight, as always, anchors him amidst the swirling currents. He watches her move behind the counter, her grace belying the years she's stood there, serving up both food and wisdom in equal measure. A nod of thanks is all he offers; it speaks volumes.

"Your gut's usually right, Nora," Tom says, the hints of a smile playing at the corners of his mouth. "If the docks are whispering secrets, I'll find out what they're saying."

"Listen closely." Nora wipes down the counter with practiced motions. "The sea has a way of changing the story with each wave."

"Let's hope it speaks more clearly than our suspects," Tom retorts, his dry wit surfacing despite the gravitas of the case at hand.

The bell above the door jingles, heralding Cassidy's entrance. She strides in, laptop cradled under her arm like a digital shield, ready to fend off the shadows with youthful exuberance. Her presence stirs the air, a fresh breeze in the warm, coffee-scented confines of the diner.

"Hey, Dad. Ready for some twenty-first-century sleuthing?" Cassidy beams, setting her technological arsenal upon a vacant table.

"Couldn't crack this one without you, Cass." Pride softens Tom's rugged features. He moves towards her, the lawyer now a father first and foremost. "What have you dug up?"

"Only the latest on every suspect's digital footprint." Cassidy flips open her laptop, fingers dancing across keys with a rhythm born of familiarity. "The internet never sleeps, and neither does your daughter's curiosity."

"Hopefully, it doesn't keep any hours past curfew," Tom quips, earning an eye roll from Cassidy that's affectionate in its exasperation.

Nora chuckles, witnessing their exchange. "You two make quite the team. Like watching a well-oiled machine."

"Or a comedy duo," Cassidy adds, winking at Nora.

"Sometimes both," Tom agrees, settling in beside his daughter. The screen glows, casting a soft light on their determined faces. Together, they dive into the digital sea, searching for the truth hidden beneath the surface.

Tom leans in, scrutinizing the constellation of data points Cassidy has gathered. The laptop screen bathes their faces in a pale blue hue, as if they are both submerged in the depths of the case itself.

"Look at this," Cassidy says, tapping a key with deliberate force. "Sarah's browser history. It's like she knew she was in danger."

"Could be paranoia, or maybe foresight," Tom muses, his eyes narrowing.

"Or maybe it's just an unhealthy obsession with true crime podcasts," she retorts, her lips twitching with a smirk that doesn't quite reach her eyes. The humor is there, but so is the gravity of their task – a balancing act she navigates with ease.

Tom chuckles, despite the grimness of their work. "Any peculiar contacts? Strange emails?"

"Nothing screams 'shady character with a murder motive,'" she replies. "But I did find encrypted messages. And guess what? They're about as secure as a diary with a 'no snooping' sticker."

"Can you crack them?" Tom asks, impressed yet unsurprised by her skills.

"Already did." Cassidy's fingers fly across the keyboard, bringing up a series of decrypted texts. "Some of these exchanges are with our friend from the docks. Looks like Sarah had more enemies than friends."

"Deep waters indeed," Tom comments, his voice a mix of admiration and concern for the dark turns their investigation takes.

"Come on, Dad, let's not get poetic. We've got a murderer to catch, not an ocean to describe," Cassidy chides gently, her wit a lighthouse guiding him back to focus.

"Right," Tom agrees, shaking his head lightly as if to rid himself of distractions. "Let's dive deeper then."

With a nod and an eye roll, Cassidy delves back into the digital depths, her father by her side. Together, they navigate the murky waters of Oakwood's secrets, each keystroke a step closer to the truth.

Nora leans over the counter, her silver hair catching the soft light as Cassidy waves a printout with enthusiasm. "Look at this," Cassidy says, pointing to a jumbled mass of numbers and letters. "It's a pattern, see? Every third letter."

"Ah," Nora murmurs, her eyes sharp despite her grandmotherly visage. "A coded message within the message."

"Exactly." Cassidy's grin is quick and proud. She thrives on puzzles, her intellect a blade slicing through confusion.

Tom watches, leaning against a red vinyl booth, arms crossed. He observes the pair – one seasoned with wisdom, the other brimming with youthful energy. Both indispensable.

"Could be a schedule," Nora suggests, tapping a finger on the paper. "Or locations."

"Or both." Cassidy's fingers tap-dance on the table, her mind racing ahead. "If we cross-reference these with dates and places..."

"Patterns emerge," Nora finishes. Their excitement is palpable, two minds in sync, weaving a tapestry of theory and deduction.

Tom smiles to himself, warmth blooming in his chest. In this quest for truth, they are more than allies; they are family. Trust is their foundation, unspoken but as real as the solid ground beneath their feet.

"Let's map it out," Cassidy says, pulling her laptop closer. The glow of the screen paints her face in cool light, her blue eyes reflecting determination.

"Good," Tom says. He steps up, joining them as they huddle around the evidence. Together, they are a united front, their shared goal shining brighter than the neon sign outside that flickers 'Open'.

"Whatever it takes," Nora adds, her voice steady. "We'll find the answers."

"Count on it," Cassidy replies, her wit dry as the coastal breeze. They dive back into the depths of the case, a beacon of camaraderie guiding their way.

The clock on the diner wall ticks in rhythm with Tom's heartbeat, a steady reminder of time slipping away. He leans back, absorbing the fragments of theory Nora and Cassidy have woven into a promising lead. The smell of coffee grounds lingers in his senses, grounding him.

"Your instincts were right," he says, nodding at Nora.

A chuckle escapes Nora's lips, her eyes crinkling with mirth. "Just doing my part. Besides, can't let you young folks have all the fun."

Tom turns to Cassidy, pride swelling in his chest. "And you, Cass. Your tech savvy might just be the ace up our sleeve."

"Comes with the territory of being a digital native," Cassidy replies, a smirk playing on her lips. "Old-school meets new-school, we're unstoppable."

Tom stands, feeling the weight of fatigue lift from his shoulders. He places a hand on both their backs—a silent thank you for their dedication. Their shared mission binds them tighter than any bloodline could.

"Let's not get ahead of ourselves," he cautions, though optimism tints his voice. "We've got work ahead. We need to see what story they tell."

"Agreed." Nora's approval is a balm to any lingering uncertainty. "We'll start first thing tomorrow. Fresh eyes, fresh perspectives."

"Tonight, we rest," Cassidy adds, closing her laptop with a decisive snap. "Tomorrow, we dissect every pixel and ink stroke."

Tom nods, his determination galvanizing into action. He thanks them again, knowing that gratitude is too small a word for the lifeline they've thrown him. They are his companions in the trenches, his allies in the skirmish against shadows.

"Sleep well," he says, stepping out into the cool night air of Oakwood. The ocean breeze whispers secrets, and Tom listens, ready to decode its messages come morning light.

The first light of dawn filters through the blinds, casting a geometric dance of shadows across Tom's face. He blinks against the intrusion, his mind already sifting through the day's agenda. The coffee pot gurgles to life in the background, a familiar comfort as he dresses in silence.

A brisk jog brings clarity, the rhythmic pounding on the pavement aligning with the beat of his heart. Oakwood stirs around him, the town shaking off slumber, ready to reveal its secrets. He spots the lighthouse in the distance, a stoic sentinel against the changing tides.

"Another day, another puzzle piece," he mutters to himself, slowing to a stop by Nora's Diner, the neon sign flickering awake.

Inside, the aroma of coffee grounds wages war against the salty tang from the docks. Tom inhales deeply, the scents grounding him. Nora nods from behind the counter, her knowing gaze taking in his renewed vigor.

"Morning, Tom. Your usual?" she calls out, her voice cutting through the morning bustle.

"Make it strong," he replies, sliding onto a stool. The vinyl squeaks under his weight, a familiar soundtrack to his routine.

He unfolds the case file, the photos and notes scattered before him like a deck of cards dealt by fate. Nora sets down a steaming mug beside him, the black liquid promising a jolt of wakefulness.

"Find anything new?" she asks, wiping her hands on a towel.

"Maybe." Tom taps a photo where a shadow lurks just beyond the crime scene tape. "Patterns within patterns."

"Sounds like you're chasing ghosts again."

"Sometimes, that's all we have." His reply is pensive, a soft chuckle escaping him despite the gravity of their conversation.

"Or maybe just chasing your own tail," Cassidy chimes in, sidling up beside him with her laptop tucked under her arm.

"Let's hope it's more productive than that." Tom takes a gulp of coffee, letting the bitterness sit on his tongue.

"Productivity is my middle name." Cassidy flips open her laptop, her fingers dancing across the keys. "Ready to dive into the digital deep?"

"Lead the way," he says, pushing aside his empty cup. With a shared nod, they plunge into the sea of data, each keystroke a stroke towards the truth hidden beneath the surface.

"Keep a lookout for anomalies," Tom instructs, scanning the lines of code reflecting off Cassidy's intent gaze.

"Anomalies are my forte," she retorts, her dry wit a beacon in the monotonous task at hand.

"Then we might just crack this yet." Tom's spirits buoy with every passing moment, the pieces inching closer to completion.

"Optimism, Dad?" Cassidy raises an eyebrow, a smile tugging at her lips. "Who are you, and what have you done with Tom Blackwell?"

"Consider it a temporary abduction." Tom smirks, turning back to his work, the quiet clack of Cassidy's keyboard a testament to their progress.

CHAPTER 5

Echoes of contention reverberate off the walls of Tom Blackwell's office, a chamber where legal battles are won and lost. Today, it hosts a different kind of struggle. Tom towers over his desk, eyes aflame with a mix of defiance and despair. Emily Foster stands her ground across from him, uniform crisp, her auburn hair a fiery contrast to the cool resolve in her gaze.

"Clara is a child, Emily. A frightened, confused child," Tom asserts, each word punctuated by a finger jabbed towards the piles of evidence scattered like a jigsaw puzzle gone awry.

"Children can be killers too, Tom." Emily's voice doesn't waver; it cuts through the tension with precision. "You know that."

Inside, though, Emily wages war with doubt. The evidence whispers guilt; her intuition screams otherwise. Her mind flips through images of Clara – small, haunted, yet with a spark that seems at odds with violence. A green-eyed stare holds steady, but her heart thuds an erratic rhythm.

"Dammit, Emily! Look at her, really look at her!" Tom's plea blankets the room. "She's no more a murderer than you or I."

"Emotion can't blind us to facts," Emily counters, but her voice falters, betraying the inner turmoil she wrestles to subdue. Her hand hovers over her phone, a lifeline to a partner who might hold the key to Clara's fate.

"Since when does justice turn a deaf ear to mercy?" Tom challenges. His grey-blue eyes, stormy seas amidst the tempest, seek an ally in Emily.

"Mercy must walk hand in hand with truth." She straightens, drawing on every ounce of strength vested in her badge.

A beat passes. Tom inhales the briny scent of Oakwood, letting the seaside calm anchor his swirling thoughts. Emily's fingers tap a staccato against her arm – Morse code for the anxious thoughts she dares not voice aloud.

"Time will tell, Sheriff Foster. Time will tell." Tom's words carry the weight of experience, seasoned with a hint of irony only Oakwood's coastal air understands. Emily nods, the ghost of a smile acknowledging the barbed olive branch.

The stalemate rests uneasy between them, two warriors with shared history now at cross purposes. Their silent agreement hangs unspoken; they'll follow the trail wherever it leads. For Clara. For justice. For Oakwood.

Tom paces, a caged protector in his own office, where the echoes of their argument still cling to the walls. Each step is a silent drumbeat, echoing his mounting frustration. His jaw sets hard as flint, fists balled up like knots in the weathered ropes that moor boats to Oakwood's docks.

The phone's ring slices through the tension. Emily snatches it up. Her spine stiffens as Jack's voice, usually a steady bass, now carries an urgent tremor. Eyes wide, she listens; the green in them sharpens—a hunter spotting a path through dense forest.

"Say again?" Her words are clipped, the authority of her badge sharpened by hope's sudden edge. The room holds its breath. Tom halts mid-stride, his protective instincts snagging on the possibility of salvation for Clara and Charles.

"New lead," she mouths across the room to him. A flicker of disbelief wars with hope behind Tom's seasoned gaze. He nods once, sharply, a general rallying at the whisper of victory.

Tom's eyes narrow, the skepticism etched in the crinkles at their corners. He watches Emily as she tilts her head, the phone cradled between shoulder and ear, her free hand slicing through the air to sketch her rising anxiety. She presses a finger against her temple, massaging it as if to coax clarity from chaos.

"Understood," she says, voice low but edged with steel. "We'll pivot immediately." Her gaze meets Tom's, searching for an echo of her own tentative hope.

He reads the play of emotions across her face — determination wrestling with doubt. His gut tightens. Is this lead the key, or just another hollow promise?

Emily hangs up, exhaling a breath she seems to have held for ages. "Jack's got something," she tells Tom, her words cautious yet carrying the weight of decision. "A witness who might blow the case wide open."

"Or send us on a wild goose chase," Tom counters, his tone flat. The lawyer in him can't help but dissect every angle, anticipate every pitfall.

"Maybe," she concedes. But then her spine straightens, green eyes bright with resolve. "I'm delaying Clara's arrest. We owe it to them to explore this."

Tom's mouth presses into a thin line. "Clara and Charles better be thanking their lucky stars you're the one wearing the badge." It's a grudging admission, but one that acknowledges her tenacity.

"Let's just focus on finding the truth, Tom." Emily's voice softens, the undercurrent of professional respect clear even as their strategies diverge.

"Truth has a way of being elusive around here," he replies, his wit dry as the autumn leaves outside. But beneath the surface, a spark of gratitude flickers. She's giving them a chance, and that's more than he expected.

Tom nods, the tightness in his jaw easing as he watches Emily's resolve ripple through her stance. The office—once an echo chamber for their discord—now houses a tentative truce. She's siding with due process, and though doubts linger like fog over Oakwood's morning shores, relief washes over him. His blue-grey eyes soften, a silent thank you communicated in that shared glance.

"I truly believe they're innocent Em, please be sure before you ruin their lives" he murmurs, the gratitude resonating in his gravelly voice, a counterpoint to the seagulls crying outside his window.

"You know I always do," she replies, the corner of her mouth lifting in a half-smile that doesn't quite chase away the tension creasing her forehead.

Their accord hangs between them, fragile but intact, as they part ways.

* * *

In the dim light of Nora's Diner, Tom convenes with Nora and Cassidy, the neon sign outside casting a red glow over their huddle. The diner, usually a hub of cheerful chatter, now serves as their war room. Silverware clinks, plates shuffle—a symphony to their strategy session.

"Every detail matters," Tom states, his focus sharp as he maps out their plan on a napkin. Cassidy leans in, her wit ready to cut through the gravity of their task. "Let's hope this isn't another breadcrumb trail leading nowhere."

"Hope is our ally today," Tom says, a rare glimmer of optimism threading his words.

Across town, at the police station, Emily stands before Jack and her team, the buzz of fluorescent lights above mirroring the urgency of her briefing. Her voice cuts clear through the room, commands delivered with the precision of an arrow finding its mark.

"Recheck alibis. Scrutinize every frame of footage. We miss nothing," she instructs, each order a step closer to unraveling The Oakwood Tragedy.

"Understood," Jack responds, his own determination mirroring hers.

As Tom and Emily mobilize their respective forces, Oakwood holds its breath, the rolling coastal mists a backdrop to a town suspended between fear and hope.

They exit their meetings, Tom's path lined with cobblestones, Emily's with the polished floors of justice. The two silhouettes departing, a visual testament to the intricate dance of their investigation.

The door to Tom's office snaps shut with a resolute click. He stands before Nora and Cassidy, his stance as firm as the convictions he carries. Salt-and-pepper hair slightly askew, a testament to the day's stress, yet his eyes burn with unwavering purpose.

"Listen up," Tom begins, voice steady, "We're missing something—a piece, a person, a motive." He plants his hands on the desk, leaning in. "Cassidy, I need you to dig into the foster home's financials. Look for anomalies, anything that doesn't add up."

Cassidy nods, her youthful energy harnessed by the gravity of her task. Her fingers itch to dance across the keyboard, to unravel the digital strands that could lead to an untold story.

"Got it, Dad. I'll see what they're hiding."

Nora, the calm amidst the storm, waits patiently. Her silver hair catches the light as she turns to face Tom, knowing her role is just as crucial.

"Nora, your place is Oakwood's pulse," Tom says, his voice softening slightly. "Talk to the regulars, glean what you can from the chatter. People reveal truths over coffee cups they'd never say to a badge."

"Consider it done," Nora replies, her tone both soothing and assertive, a gentle force to be reckoned with.

Across town, in the stark sterility of the precinct, Emily stands tall, a beacon of authority. Jack and the officers hang on her every directive, ready to spring into action. The fluorescent hum underscores her words, adding gravity to each command.

"We've got a new lead," Emily announces, green eyes alight with resolve. "A potential witness came forward—saw something unusual near the docks the night Morgan was killed. Jack, take two officers, canvas the area. Find anyone who might have seen our ghost."

"Right away, Sheriff," Jack affirms, already mentally mapping out his approach, the team coalescing around this fresh avenue of inquiry.

"Everyone else, we re-interview the neighbors. If someone knows something, and we need to uncover it," Emily continues, her presence commanding the space, drawing forth effort and diligence from her team.

"Understood, Sheriff Foster," the officers chorus, spurred into motion by her unwavering commitment to justice.

Tom's office now echoes with silence, the plans set into motion. He gazes out the window at the cobblestone streets of Oakwood below, where shadows lengthen as the sun dips toward the horizon. His mind races with strategies and contingencies, the weight of innocence resting on his next moves.

Emily exits the briefing room, her stride confident, her path clear. She passes through the station, her senses tuned to the subtle symphony of law and order—the clack of keyboards, the shuffle of papers, the murmurs of duty-bound voices.

Both teams, fueled by the drive of their leaders, delve into Oakwood's secrets. Each clue, each anomaly is a step closer to piercing the veil of The Oakwood Tragedy, and with dogged persistence, Tom and Emily press on.

❋ ❋ ❋

Tom strides down the docks, the echo of his footsteps a sharp clatter against the hushed rolling of Oakwood's evening tide. His jaw sets firm, thoughts churning like the restless sea as he rounds a corner—and there she stands.

Emily pauses, mid-step, her green eyes locking with Tom's in a silent clash of wills. For an electric moment, the world shrinks to the space between them, charged with unsaid words and unyielded ground. Then, without a word, they brush past each other, their resolve as palpable as the coastal breeze that slips through the open window.

"Ah, the fabled Sheriff Foster," Tom murmurs under his breath, the hint of a smirk tugging at the corner of his mouth. "I'm more likely to find a clam with its shell wide open."

Back in the safety of his office after his walk, Tom spots Nora and Cassidy poring over files, their faces etched with concentration. He clears his throat, easing the tension with the comfort of his presence.

"Remember, ladies, when chasing leads, make sure you're not just fishing for red herrings." Cassidy rolls her eyes but a grin betrays her fondness for her father's levity.

"Red herrings, Dad? Really?" Cassidy quips, her sarcasm a deft dance with Tom's humor.

"Only if they lead us to the big fish," Nora chimes in, her smile reflecting the flicker of hope that still burns in the depths of this murky case.

"God you two are like a pun factory" smirked Cassidy.

* * *

Emily strides through the precinct, the click of her boots on the linoleum floor punctuates the air like a metronome counting down to justice. Officers and deputies part before her like the sea, sensing the tide of her determination.

"Let's start with the neighbors," she commands, eyes scanning the latest reports. Her team falls in line, a parade of resolve as they head toward the interrogation room. She sifts through papers, each word scrutinized under her analytical gaze, her mind a chessboard where pieces of testimony and evidence shift and realign with every new revelation.

"Keep the questions tight. We're looking for inconsistencies, not life stories," she instructs, her voice clear and devoid of doubt. Jack nods, his own resolve an echo of hers, knowing full well the weight of what hangs in the balance.

* * *

In a small, crowded room at the public library, Tom leans over microfiche reels, the whirring sound filling the space as images flicker across the screen. He squints, absorbing dates, names, and events that paint the history of the foster home—a tableau of care and crisis.

"Look at this," Tom mutters, fingers tracing a line of text. "A custody battle five years back. Might explain a few things." His jaw sets, a silent vow etched into the lines around his mouth. Each discovery, a stepping stone in the murky waters he navigates, brings him closer to the truth he seeks.

"Five years is a long time to hold a grudge," Cassidy muses from beside him, her curiosity piqued by the narrative unfolding.

"Or just enough time to plan the perfect crime," Tom replies, the corner of his mouth lifting ever so slightly. It's a grim humor that keeps the shadows at bay, a spark in the darkness of their task.

* * *

Back at the station, Emily stands behind the two-way mirror, studying the face of the neighbor being questioned. A muscle twitches in her cheek as she watches, her gut a barometer for deceit. Each answer, each evasion adds a piece to the puzzle she's assembling in her head.

"Push on the night of the murder," she says suddenly, her intuition flaring. "There's something not right there."

* * *

Tom, meanwhile, flips through pages of financial records, his eyes sharp as talons. "Money always leaves a trail," he intones, the phrase a mantra against confusion. A series of transactions stands out, a pattern amidst chaos, and he feels the rush of adrenaline that comes with a lead worth pursuing.

"Could be our golden ticket," Nora suggests, leaning in to study the figures. Tom gives a single nod, the closest admission of hope he'll allow himself in these moments of conjecture.

"Or another wild goose chase," he counters, but the energy in the room has shifted. They can all sense it—the scent of possibility, elusive yet intoxicating, drawing them deeper into the heart of the mystery.

Both teams, though operating separately, are united in their quest. The evening light wanes, casting long shadows across Oakwood, but within the walls of the precinct and the hushed corners of the library, the search for truth knows no rest.

* * *

The clock's steady tick in Tom's office merges with the pulse throbbing at his temples. He pores over the foster home's ledger, each entry a breadcrumb on a trail that winds and twists through shadowed woods of motive. His fingers pause; there's an anomaly in the numbers, a break in the pattern that could mean everything—or nothing.

"Damned if I let this slip through," he mutters, the words barely audible.

In another part of Oakwood, Emily stands in the dim glow of streetlights, phone pressed to her ear. Her breath fogs in the cool night air, a visual echo of her mounting tension. She listens, her mind racing as Jack's voice crackles through, words painting a picture that could flip their world upside down.

"Are you certain?" she asks, green eyes narrowing against the dark.

"Positive," Jack replies. "It changes everything."

Back in his office, Tom lets out a low whistle, the sound cutting through silence. He leans back, chair creaking under the weight of implications heavy as anvils. A new piece of the puzzle slides into place, the edges sharp with potential.

"Looks like this game's not over yet," he says, a wry smile tugging at his lips.

Their paths draw inexorably closer, two currents in a churning sea destined to collide. In the hush of impending storm, Tom gathers his papers, the lantern of his intellect burning bright against the murk of uncertainty. Emily ends her call, every fiber coiled tight with the promise of the lead Jack has secured.

"Time to see where this takes us," she whispers to the night, her determination a beacon that refuses to be snuffed out by doubt.

Their steps echo in the hallway, a silent dance as they move toward an intersection of fate. The briefest of glances is exchanged, electric with unspoken questions, before they continue on—two solitary figures united by the gravity of the truth they seek.

"Tick tock, murderer," Tom calls softly to the shadows, a playful lilt to his tone that belies the steel underneath.

"Your time's running out," Emily adds from afar, her words a vow etched in resolve.

Oakwood holds its breath, the coastal hamlet wrapped in the anticipation of what dawn might reveal.

CHAPTER 6

Tom Blackwell pushes open the door to his office, the familiar creak a testament to the years spent within these walls. He halts, finding Clara Leblanc perched on the edge of a leather chair, her posture as stiff as the spines of the legal tomes lining the bookshelves. She's a striking figure amid the mundane: dark hair framing her face in defiance, eyes glinting with a mix of wariness and resolve.

"Mr. Blackwell," she begins, her voice betraying none of the tumult surely churning inside her. "I need your help."

"Clearly," Tom observes, setting aside his briefcase. His eyes soften. The crisp Oakwood air couldn't dilute the tension that clung to her like a second skin. "You're not here to discuss the weather, I presume?"

Clara's lips twitch, almost a smile, but it's gone before it can bloom. She shakes her head, clutching a worn backpack to her chest—a makeshift shield. "It's about Charles and me. We have nowhere to go after...after what happened to Mrs. Reynolds."

The gravity of the Oakwood Tragedy bears down on the room. Tom nods, understanding. "You'll stay with us," he says, simple and final. Her eyes widen, defenses faltering for a heartbeat. "No arguments, Clara. You and Charles are under my wing now."

The ride to Tom's home, a quaint clapboard nestled amongst hydrangeas and white picket fences, passes in silence. Clara's gaze flits between passing landmarks, each one a potential harbinger of either sanctuary or further despair.

They arrive, and Cassidy greets them at the door, her own grey-blue eyes reflecting her father's determination. "Hey," she chirps, ushering them inside with an enthusiasm that belies the seriousness of their intrusion into her life.

"Clara, Charles, this is Cassidy," Tom introduces, watching the dynamics unfold. "She's going to be your crash course in all things 'normal teenager' while you're here."

Cassidy grins, extending a hand first to Clara, then to Charles. "Welcome to the chaos." Her offer is genuine, a lifeline thrown with the promise of friendship.

"Chaos is her middle name, unfortunately" Tom quips, earning an eye roll from his daughter. He clears his throat, adopting the solemnity befitting a guardian. "We're here for you both, to make sure you're safe and—to the best of our ability—happy."

"Happy's a tall order," Clara replies, a wisp of her guarded humor surfacing. "But safe would be a good start."

"Safe is a start," Tom agrees. He watches as Cassidy leads them through the threshold, into the unknown yet oddly comforting embrace of family.

Emily Foster stands amidst the strewn contents of her overnight bag, as she repacks each item. The fabric of her uniform brushes against her skin, a reminder of the duty that calls her. Each fold of clothing, each tuck of personal effects, whispers of the chasm widening between her and Tom. She pauses, green eyes tracing the familiar contours of her apartment—the refuge that has become both synonymous with solitary confinement. She zips the bag with a finality that echoes in the empty space.

"Oh Em," she murmurs to herself, a mantra to quell the tempest of emotions threatening to capsize her resolve. Her badge, pinned to her chest, seems to weigh heavier today, its luster dulled by the shadow of Oakwood's tragedy. With one last glance at the reflection of her determined visage in the mirror, she steps out, locking the door on personal turmoil to embrace the clarity of her professional identity.

The police station hums with the subtle electricity of purpose. Emily strides through the corridors, her boots clicking a rhythm that announces her arrival long before she reaches Jack Turner's desk. His stocky frame is bent over paperwork, the furrow of his brow indicative of the same urgency that fuels her own quest for answers.

"Jack," she says, voice unwavering, "we need to talk."

He looks up, dark eyes meeting hers, an unspoken understanding passing between them. They retreat to the quiet of an interrogation room, a sterile sanctuary devoid of distractions.

"Clara and Charles, they were our initial suspects," Emily begins, laying out the photos and reports like a grim mosaic on the table. "But it's not adding up. Something's off."

"Pressure's mounting from above," Jack interjects, his words cut from granite, "but we're not playing politics with this one."

"Never have," she responds, a wry twist to her lips. "We follow the evidence, wherever it leads. Even if it takes us down paths less traveled by the mayor's office."

"Especially then," Jack agrees, his nod curt, decisive.

"Let's dive back in. Fresh eyes might catch what we missed the first time around." Emily's gaze drifts to the window, where the town of Oakwood basks in deceptive tranquility. Gulls cry out, oblivious to the undercurrents eroding the shores of justice beneath them.

"Back to square one," Jack says, but there's no defeat in his voice, only the grit of resolve.

"Back to square one," she echoes, rolling up the sleeves of her uniform. There's work to be done, and for Sheriff Emily Foster, the pursuit of truth knows no rest.

The morning sun casts a sharp-edged shadow across Tom Blackwell's desk, where Clara Leblanc sits, an island of defiance in a sea of legal tomes and case files. Tom leans back against the doorframe, studying her silhouette, the sunlight igniting edges of determination lining her posture.

"Clara," he starts, his voice steady as the tide, "I know trust doesn't come easy. It's like trying to catch smoke with your bare hands." He steps into the room, the scent of salt from the Seaside Haven clinging to his jacket. "But I'm here, for you and Charles."

She looks up, her dark eyes a mix of skepticism and hope. A silent beat passes before she nods, ever so slightly.

He pulls up a chair, the legs scraping gently against the wooden floor. His grey-blue eyes lock onto hers, carrying the weight of his own past. "I've walked a mile or two in shoes that pinch, Clara. As a single father, every day was a tightrope walk."

Her guard lowers, just a fraction, at the admission. "How did you manage?" Her voice is a whisper, barely there, yet it carves through the distance between them.

"By never looking down," he says with a half-smile, his dry wit a brief flicker in the solemn office. "And by remembering that sometimes, the only way out is through."

The door creaks open and Cassidy, the embodiment of youthful energy and determination, bursts in, her wavy brown hair swaying. "Dad, got a minute?" The question is rhetorical; her laptop already flips open, a dance of code and data on the screen.

"Always for you, Cass," Tom replies, turning his attention to his daughter, whose presence seems to sweep the heaviness from the room.

"Jonathan Reynolds," Cassidy begins, fingers flying over the keyboard with a pianist's grace. "His digital footprint's muddier than a backwoods trail after a storm." She squints at the display, lines of concentration etching her forehead.

"Meaning?" Tom prompts, glancing from his daughter to Clara, who watches, intrigued despite herself.

"Meaning our Mr. Reynolds has been scrubbing his online presence clean. But" – Cassidy grins, triumphant – "he missed a spot or two."

"Good work, Cass" – pride softens Tom's features – "keep digging. We might just find the thread that unravels this whole mess."

"Like a sweater snagged on a fence," Cassidy quips, her eyes alight with the thrill of the chase. She taps away, the quiet click-clack of keys punctuating their shared resolve.

"Looks like we have a lead," Tom murmurs, more to himself than to anyone else. A lead that could either be a beacon of truth or a siren leading them further into the depths of the Oakwood Tragedy.

Tom leans back, eyes tracing the spines of law books that line his office walls. Clara sits across from him, her posture stiff, every line of her body coiled like a spring. A chessboard between them, pieces at play in a game too real.

"Start from the beginning," Tom says, voice steady as a drumbeat. "The foster home."

Clara's gaze hardens, dark hair tumbling over one eye as she recounts the tale. "Morgan was kind, but the house... it was weird." Her fingers tap a rhythm on the armrest, recounting silent screams and stifled dreams.

"Weird huh? Tom muses, thumbing the edge of his desk. He ponders aloud, "Any disputes with locals? Unusual visitors?"

"Arguments were plenty," Clara admits, "mostly about money or the kids. Morgan's ex, Jonathan, he'd show up sometimes— angry, unpredictable."

"Jonathan," Tom echoes, Cassidy's earlier revelation flashing in his mind.

Meanwhile, Emily strides through Oakwood's heart, Sheriff's badge a gleam under the sun. Jack Turner, tall and hawkish beside her, scans faces as they approach Nora's Diner.

"Remember," Emily instructs, her eyes mirrors of determination, "listen more than talk."

Jack nods, and they push through the diner door, bell jingling an announcement. Inside, the aroma of coffee battles the tang of sea air for dominance. The duo zeroes in on a group of fishermen, their conversation ebbing as law enforcement approaches.

"Morning, gents," Emily greets, her tone a blend of honey and steel. "Mind if we join you?"

Suspicion flickers in the fishermen's eyes, wary of the intrusion. But they nod, shuffling to make space. Jack slides into the booth, spiral notebook at the ready.

"Regarding Morgan Reynolds..." Emily starts, probing gently.

One fisherman, grizzled and weathered, locks eyes with her. "That tragedy?" he grumbles, voice gravelly as the shore. "Nothing but sorrow for those kids."

"Anyone acting strange around her place?" Jack interjects, pencil poised.

"Strange is as common as clams here," another quips, eliciting a round of chuckles.

"Specific strange," Jack specifies, a wry smile tugging at the corner of his mouth.

Back at the office, Tom and Clara are deep in the labyrinth of motive and opportunity. Tom's mind races, thoughts flickering like shadows in the fading light.

"Could be anyone with a grudge," Clara suggests, her voice betraying a sliver of fear.

"Or someone hiding in plain sight," Tom adds, his intuition a compass pointing toward unseen truths.

"Plain sight," Clara repeats, contemplation dawning like a slow sunrise.

"Sometimes, the darkest secrets are nestled in the brightest places," Tom offers, a hint of sardonic wisdom coloring his words.

In Nora's Diner, resistance crumbles like stale bread. A lead emerges: a stranger, asking questions about the foster home days before the murder.

"Interesting," Emily murmurs, filing away the information like a precious gem.

"Could be nothing," Jack cautions, ever the skeptic.

"Could or could not, but it's something," Emily counters, her green eyes reflecting the fire of pursuit.

As the interviews draw to a close, Emily and Jack step out into the daylight, the weight of their task as heavy as the ocean's depths. Yet their resolve stands firm, a lighthouse against the encroaching fog of uncertainty.

————

The clinking of silverware punctuates the evening air, an ordinary sound that masks the tension at Tom's dining table. Four figures huddle over plates of steaming lasagna, the aroma rich with herbs and tomatoes—a stark contrast to the undercurrent of worry that lies between them.

Cassidy chatters about school projects, her voice a bright note trying to stitch normalcy into their strained dinner. Clara's posture is rigid, her fork navigating her meal with mechanical precision. Young Charles' eyes dart from face to face, searching for signs of stability in the uncertain landscape of adult concerns.

"Clara," Tom says, his tone even, "there's no need to look over your shoulder here." His gaze is steady, offering an anchor in the roiling sea of fear. "You and Charles are safe here."

Clara lifts her eyes, meets Tom's assurance with a hesitant nod. The vulnerability in her expression tugs at something deep within him.

"Thank you, Tom," she murmurs, her voice a whisper against the tide of chaos that brought them here. "But how can we ever feel truly safe again?"

"By sticking together," Cassidy interjects, her youthful optimism defiant in the face of darkness. "Like a team, right?"

"Exactly," Tom confirms, allowing a flicker of pride for his daughter to warm his features. "And we're a pretty formidable team."

As laughter brushes the table like a balm, Oakwood's quaint charm peeks through the windows, the gentle lapping of the seaside waves a reminder of the world outside this sanctuary. But beneath the town's picturesque veneer, secrets fester like hidden rot.

Meanwhile, Emily stands by the cruiser, phone pressed to her ear, Jack's attentive silhouette beside her. The informant's words crackle through the line—a tip, a clue, a whisper of possibility. Her pulse quickens; opportunity beckons.

"Where?" Emily asks, urgency threading her tone. She catches Jack's eye, signals the gravity of the lead with a sharp nod.

"Dockside warehouse," the voice on the other end hisses, the static of secrecy in every syllable. "Midnight exchange. Might be what you're looking for."

"Got it," she says, the line dead before the echo of her words fades. Her green eyes glint, a reflection of the hunt they're embroiled in.

"Let's roll," Jack says, his skepticism shelved for the moment.

They slip into the cruiser, the engine's growl a promise of pursuit as they tear away from the curb. The coastal hamlet blurs past— their lighthouse of justice cutting through the fog of deceit.

"Could be a trap," Jack muses, hands tight on the wheel.

"Or our best shot yet," Emily counters, her focus laser sharp. Their shared determination fuels them forward, a tandem force against what threatens Oakwood's light.

Tom's office door in the home slams open with an urgency that sets the papers on his desk into a frenzied dance. Cassidy is a step behind, her gaze locked on the screen of her laptop as if she's unraveling the very fabric of the world. "Dad," she says, her voice a mix of excitement and dread, "I've got something."

"Spill it," Tom commands, his attention snapping to his daughter like a magnet.

"Bank records," Cassidy reveals, her fingers flying over the keys. "There's a pattern of payments to a shell company, one that intersects with Jonathan's finances."

"An accomplice?" Tom's eyes narrow, the pieces of the puzzle clicking together in his mind.

"Looks like." She swivels the laptop toward him. Numbers and names leap out, damning evidence in digital form.

Tom stands, chair scraping back with a harsh screech. "Let's pay Jonathan a visit."

* * *

Jonathan's temporary home looms before them, a facade of respectability that can't mask the scent of secrets within. Tom's knock is a hammer strike against the silence, the sound echoing ominously.

The door swings open, and there stands Jonathan, his smile a well-rehearsed lie. Hello there, what brings you here?"

"Cut the charm, Reynolds," Tom says, stepping inside uninvited. "We know about the payments."

Jonathan's smile falters, a crack in his armor. "Allegations without proof—"

"Save it," Cassidy interjects, her voice steel wrapped in velvet.

"We're not here to debate."

"Who's your friend, Jonathan?" Tom's question is a pointed blade.

"Accusations like these could ruin a man," Jonathan retorts, attempting to regain control.

"Only if they're true," Tom shoots back.

* * *

Across town, the sirens' wail cuts through the night, a harbinger of grim tidings. Emily and Jack arrive at the dockside warehouse, their steps quick and purposeful. The moon casts long shadows over the scene, its light insufficient against the darkness of their discovery.

"Over here," a voice calls from the shadows. It's Sergeant Turner, his face etched with concern.

Emily's heart sinks as they approach. There, under the stark beam of a flashlight, lies the body of their witness, life extinguished too soon. The air hangs heavy with the tang of salt and loss.

"Damn it," she curses under her breath, her hopes dashed upon the rocky shore of reality.

"Could've told us everything," Jack murmurs, the gravity of their setback weighing on him like chains.

"Jonathan's accomplice," Emily whispers, "just went up in smoke."

"Back to square one," Jack states, but the set of Emily's shoulders speaks of her unyielding resolve.

"Or we dig deeper," she replies, her gaze already searching the horizon for the faintest glint of truth.

Tom slumps against the cold metal of his desk, fingers threading through salt-and-pepper strands. Cassidy sits across from him, her laptop's glow casting stark light on her determined features. Their eyes meet, sharing a wordless conversation charged with frustration and fear.

"Hit a dead end," Tom mutters, the words tasting like defeat. Cassidy's fingers pause their dance over the keyboard.

"Maybe not," she counters, though doubt shadows her tone. "There's always another angle, right?" Her optimism is a thin veil over worry for Clara and Charles – their safety now hangs by a thread.

"Another angle," Tom echoes, skepticism hitching a ride on hope. "Sounds good when you say it."

Cassidy offers a hollow chuckle, the sound brittle in the thick air of tension. She leans back, considering the electronic maze before her. "What if we loop back? Check the foster home's accounts again?"

"Grasping at straws..." Tom begins, but his gaze sharpens. "Do it, what have we got to lose."

Meanwhile, Emily strides into Nora's Diner, Jack on her heels. The place buzzes with Oakwood's nightly rituals, oblivious to the tragedy unfolding beyond its walls. They slide into a booth, red vinyl squeaking under their weight.

"Back to square one," Jack says, thumbing through his notes. A heavy sigh escapes him, nearly lost amid the clatter of dishes and murmur of conversations.

"Square one is a place to stand," Emily retorts, her resolve as steady as the lighthouse guiding ships home. "We just need a new direction."

"Revisit old witnesses?" Jack suggests, the wheels turning behind his furrowed brow.

"Turn over every stone they've ever walked on," she insists, her green eyes reflecting the neon sign outside. "Someone knows something, and I intend to shake it loose."

They hunker down, piecing together fragments of interviews, cross-referencing statements, looking for the crack in the facade. Every so often, Emily's gaze drifts toward the window, where moonlight dances on cobblestones, as if whispering secrets just out of reach.

"Let's talk to that cashier again, the one who saw Jonathan near the docks," she decides, tapping a finger on the laminated menu.

"Think she held back?" Jack asks, already gathering his things.

"Intuition," Emily says, sliding out of the booth. "Sometimes it's all we've got."

"Then let's hope your gut's as sharp as your aim," Jack quips, following her out into the night.

CHAPTER 7

Tom Blackwell's office, a fortress of legal tomes and the detritus of countless cases solved and pending, now resembles the aftermath of an intellectual storm. He sits with his back ramrod straight, rifling through documents like a cardsharp on a winning streak. His daughter Cassidy leans over a pile of files, her fingers dance across the pages with youthful dexterity. Nora Thompson perches on the edge of a chair, her eagle eyes missing nothing.

"Here," Cassidy says, tapping a finger on a page. "This entry for groceries—it doesn't add up." Her brows knit together, a mirror of her father's focus.

"Good catch," Tom replies, without looking up from his own papers. "Nora, remember when you said something seemed off with the home's budget?"

Nora nods, her silver hair catching the light. "I did. And it wasn't just the numbers. It was the feeling in my gut."

"Let's expand our search," Tom suggests. "Get a sense of the context beyond these walls."

"Should we consider talking to the old staff? The neighbors?" Nora's voice holds the warmth of her diner, but her suggestion cuts through the room like a chef's knife.

"Exactly what I was thinking." Tom finally lifts his gaze, his eyes a stormy sea of thought. "Cassidy, can you reach out to them?"

"Can do," Cassidy affirms with a quick nod, her laptop already open and waiting. Her fingers fly over the keys, a maestro at play. "I'll scour social media, public records, forums—you name it."

"Keep an eye out for anything... peculiar," Tom instructs, his words deliberate, carrying the weight of experience.

"Define peculiar," Cassidy quips, a playful smirk on her lips.

"Anything that doesn't belong in a sleepy coastal town like Oakwood," he answers with a rare half-smile that crinkles the corners of his eyes.

"Got it. Peculiarities are my specialty," Cassidy responds, the click-clack of her keyboard punctuating her enthusiasm.

As they delve deeper into the labyrinth of facts and conjectures, the office fades away, leaving only the heart of the mystery pulsing before them. Each clue uncovered, every inconsistency highlighted adds a piece to the puzzle of the Oakwood Tragedy. In the symphony of their investigation, the notes of truth begin to emerge, slowly crafting a melody that could lead to justice for Morgan Reynolds and redemption for Clara and Charles Leblanc.

The door to the interrogation room swings open, and Jonathan Reynolds steps through its frame, a mask of composed grief etched on his face. Emily watches him, her green eyes sharp as she notes the calculated smoothness in his stride. Her fingers tap an irregular beat on the oak table, betraying no hint of her skepticism.

"Jonathan," she begins, her voice measured, "thank you for cooperating."

"Of course," he replies, settling into the chair across from her. "Anything for Morgan." His tone drips with feigned sincerity, a veneer of the grieving ex-husband.

Jack Turner stands against the wall, arms folded, his presence a solid anchor in the room. He scrutinizes Jonathan, no detail escaping his perceptive gaze. The sergeant's stance rigid, his mind already sifting through the man's words before they even leave his lips.

"Let's talk about the evening Morgan was killed," Emily prods gently, yet her eyes betray the steel behind the question.

Jonathan recounts his alibi, a rehearsed tale that dances around the edges of plausibility. Emily's intuition prickles; something about his story doesn't sit right with the briny air of Oakwood.

Outside, Tom strides toward the local library, his jaw set. The quaint building, with its promise of archived truths, beckons him. He pushes open the heavy wooden door, the scent of old paper and ink greeting him like an old friend. The librarian nods a silent welcome, recognizing the determined look of a man on a quest.

Tom moves through rows of musty shelves, his fingers trailing over the spines of history. Oakwood's past whispers to him, tales of joy and sorrow living side by side. He halts at a section where local newspapers are preserved in bound volumes, their yellowed pages guardians of secrets long forgotten.

"Looking for anything specific?" the librarian inquires, her voice a soft intrusion.

"Past incidents involving one Jonathan Reynolds," Tom says, his words efficient, leaving no room for further questions.

"Ah," she murmurs, tapping at the computer. "I'll see what we can find."

As the printer hums to life, Tom's grey-blue eyes scan each line of text with precision, searching for the thread that might unravel Jonathan's carefully woven narrative. Each article, each police report he examines, adds depth to the portrait he's painting—a mosaic of charm and shadows.

Back at the station, Emily concludes the interview. "We may need to speak again," she says, her tone implying it's not a request.

"Understandable," Jonathan agrees smoothly, standing. His dark blue eyes lock with Emily's for a moment too long, a silent challenge.

"Jack, walk Mr. Reynolds out, please," Emily orders, already contemplating her next move.

"Will do, Sheriff," Jack responds, ushering the enigmatic man from the room.

Emily's thoughts churn like the coastal tide—doubt and certainty colliding. She needs more, but what? The answer lies beyond the initial evidence, Emily is sure of it.

At the library, Tom stumbles upon an article, his pulse quickening. A past altercation, Jonathan's name in the mix. Not conclusive, but a sliver of doubt wedges itself into the case's foundation. Tom folds the printout, tucking it into his jacket pocket. It's a lead, and in Oakwood, leads are as precious as daylight during the shortening autumn days.

"Thank you," he nods to the librarian, his expression giving nothing away.

"Good luck," she offers, sensing the undercurrent of urgency.

Tom exits, the setting sun casting long shadows over Oakwood's quaint charm. The pieces are moving, and somewhere between the lines of official accounts and hushed town gossip, truth awaits.

"Time to dig deeper," Tom mutters to himself, determination fueling his stride.

Tom's office, a bastion of legal prowess amidst the seaside serenity of Oakwood, thrums with activity. Cassidy hunches over her laptop, fingers dancing across the keyboard, eyes narrowing as lines of financial data scroll down her screen. The scent of aged paper and determination fills the air, mingling with the faint tang of the ocean drifting through an open window.

"Got something," Cassidy announces, without looking up from her screen. Her tone, usually peppered with humor, carries a weight of severity.

Tom leans in, his rugged face etched with focus. He scans the figures Cassidy points out—unusual withdrawals, deposits that don't add up. "This doesn't look like pocket change for a pack of gum," he quips, despite the gravity of the discovery.

"Unless it's spearmint-flavored gold," Cassidy retorts, her quick-witted sarcasm not quite masking her concern. She swivels the laptop toward him, revealing a spiderweb of transactions crisscrossing over state lines, all roads leading to Jonathan Reynolds.

"Any ties to the foster home?" Tom asks, already knowing the answer he wants isn't at their fingertips—not yet.

"That's my next deep dive," Cassidy replies with a determined glint in her blue eyes. She's ready to plunge into the digital depths, chase the elusive truth that lurks beneath surface appearances.

"Be thorough," Tom instructs, his voice steady, betraying none of his mounting intrigue. "We need concrete connections, not just suspicious cash flows."

"Like finding a needle in a haystack that's also a labyrinth," Cassidy says, cracking her knuckles before returning to her hunt.

"Except you're wielding a magnet and a map," Tom counters, his dry wit surfacing even amid the tension.

Cassidy's research skills are a beacon, piercing through the fog of uncertainty. She combs through social media, public records, anything that could bind Jonathan Reynolds to the foster home, to Morgan's untimely demise.

"Here," she eventually breathes out, triumph mixed with dismay. A photo surfaces on her screen, Jonathan at a charity event for the foster home, Morgan beside him, both smiling for the camera—a moment frozen, now laced with dark undertones.

"Keep going, Cass," Tom urges, his jaw set. Time is their relentless adversary, and every second counts.

Cassidy nods, diving back into the digital sea. Her father watches, pride swelling in his chest for his daughter's tenacity. They are a team, united by blood and the unshakeable need for justice. And as the sun dips below the horizon, painting the sky with streaks of fiery orange, they continue their quest, knowing that each clue uncovered brings them one step closer to piercing the heart of Oakwood's tragedy.

Emily strides through Oakwood's police station, her green eyes sharpening as she absorbs the latest reports. Jack thumbs through yet another list of witness statements. The din of ringing phones and conversations fills the air.

"Dead end," Jack mutters, tossing aside a paper with a flick of his wrist. "Every lead we follow, it's like chasing our own tail."

"They can't hide forever," Emily counters, her voice a blend of assurance and impatience. Her fingers drum on the desk, betraying her frustration. She senses they're missing a piece, a critical sliver of truth.

A call from the mayor's office cuts through the buzz. Demands for an arrest — specifically, the Leblanc children — punctuate the conversation. Emily presses the receiver tighter to her ear, her jaw setting. The political pressure is a vise, tightening with each passing hour.

"Tell the mayor we're working on it," she says, but her tone suggests she's speaking to a wall, not an aide.

❈ ❈ ❈

The door to Tom's office creaks open, revealing stacks of files and documents that cascade across every surface. Tom, Nora, and Cassidy step inside, their silhouettes framed by the golden glow of the setting sun.

"Let's start with the neighbors," Tom suggests, flipping through his notes. His voice is steady, but there's an undercurrent of urgency that belies his calm demeanor.

Nora nods, her mind already sifting through potential questions. They need answers, solid ones, not just more speculation.

"Mrs. Henderson next door always had an eye on this place," Cassidy volunteers. "If anyone knows the comings and goings, it'd be her."

"Then let's pay Mrs. Henderson a visit," Tom decides, leading the way out of the office.

❊ ❊ ❊

The trio stands on Mrs. Henderson's porch, the ocean's briny scent mingling with the aroma of old roses from her garden. A timid knock on the door, and moments later, it swings open to reveal a face marred by time but sharp with curiosity.

"Mrs. Henderson, we're looking into the foster home..." Nora begins, her tone gentle yet probing.

"Terrible business, that murder," Mrs. Henderson clucks, ushering them inside. The living room is a shrine to bygone eras, doilies and faded photographs commanding attention.

"Did you notice anything unusual around the foster home?" Tom inquires, his gaze direct.

"Always something off about that place," the old woman confides, leaning closer. "Children looking sullen, workers turning over faster than pancakes at Nora's Diner."

"Neglect?" Cassidy's question hangs in the air, weighted with implications.

"More than just neglect, dear," Mrs. Henderson affirms, a tremor of indignation in her voice. "Heard cries at night, I did. And Morgan... well, she was no saint herself."

Tom exchanges a glance with Nora, both sensing the pattern unfolding.

"Thank you, Mrs. Henderson," Nora says, her gratitude genuine. "You've been very helpful."

"Speak up when things ain't right," the old woman advises, her eyes meeting theirs with a glint of resolve.

As they leave the doorstep, the cold breeze carries whispers of secrets long buried. Tom tucks his hands into his coat pockets, feeling the weight of the task ahead. The foster home's facade of care has cracked, revealing a grim reality beneath.

"Next, we talk to the former employees," he states, determination etched in his features.

"Ready when you are," Cassidy replies, her blue eyes reflecting the twilight sky, a mirror of resolve. Together, they step back into the labyrinth.

" And I think I'm gonna take a close look at Jonathan's movements the next few days" Tom states, " You guys try and find someone who will talk to us."

Tom follows Jonathan, with nothing of interest all day, in fact he was getting bored, until he stopped by the Seaside Haven. Tom remembers how he and Emily once went undercover there one night and smiled. That smile quickly faded though.

Emily strides into The Seaside Haven as the clink of the door's bell announcing her presence. Autumn light filters through the windows, casting a warm glow on the mahogany bar where Jonathan Reynolds leans casually. His deep blue eyes catch the sunlight, and for a moment, he appears almost ethereal.

"Jonathan," she calls out, assertive, every bit the town's sheriff.

"Emily." His voice is smooth, a river of honey that could sweeten the most bitter coffee at Nora's Diner across the square. "To what do I owe the pleasure?"

She takes a seat, angled to face him, her green eyes fixed like laser sights. "Just a chat."

"Always a delight," he replies, his charm offensive in full swing.

Tom watches from a distance, a silent sentinel outside The Seaside Haven. He notes the subtle shift in Emily's posture — a softening, perhaps? Or merely strategy? Jonathan's charisma weaves through the conversation, palpable even through the pane of glass that separates them.

"Did Morgan ever mention feeling... unsafe?" Emily probes, searching for cracks in the facade.

Jonathan pauses, a masterful stroke to feign reflection. "Morgan had her demons, but fear? well not that she showed." A perfect response, Tom muses, admiring despite himself.

"Demons," Emily echoes, skeptical yet intrigued.

"Indeed," Jonathan affirms, lacing his words with enigma.

Tom shifts, restless, his grey-blue eyes tracing Jonathan's every gesture. He catches a flicker of something — a glance, a touch — between them. It gnaws at him, this dance.

"Pressure's mounting for an arrest," Emily confesses, leaning in closer than necessary.

"Is that so?" Jonathan's eyebrow arches, a sculpted line of intrigue.

"Indeed," she mirrors his earlier reply, a playful tilt to her lips.

"Careful, Emily," Tom whispers to himself, the weight of concern pressing against his chest. He knows the game they play, a high-stakes chess match where hearts and truths are the currency.

"Pressure can burst pipes or make diamonds," Jonathan quips, leaning back with the ease of a man unburdened by conscience.

"Which are you, Jonathan?" Emily challenges, a spark of defiance igniting behind her gaze.

"Let's hope for diamonds," he responds with a sly grin, unaware of Tom's hidden scrutiny.

In the waning light, Tom battles the urge to intervene, to shatter the spellbinding exchange. He remains unseen, a ghost haunting the periphery, collecting the silent confessions that hang in the air.

"Another meeting?" Jonathan suggests, his invitation wrapped in velvet tones.

"Perhaps," Emily replies, non-committal yet charmed, her resolve a flickering flame in the coastal breeze.

"Until then," he says, standing with the grace of a cat, offering his hand.

"Until then," she agrees, and their hands meet—a handshake or a caress?

As she exits, Tom retreats further into the shadows, his presence an unspoken question mark punctuating the scene. The rendezvous has ended, but the investigation—and the game—press onward.

The glow of the computer across Cassidy's intense gaze, fingers flying over keys. She pauses, leans in; a pattern emerges from the digital chaos.

"Gotcha," she murmurs, the two words a victory cry in the silent room.

Tom hovers, a sentinel framed by the doorway. His daughter's triumphant whisper draws his attention away from the myriad documents that crowd his desk.

"Talk to me, Cass."

She pivots in her chair, face illuminated by revelation. "Jonathan's cash flows intersect with some shady players. Looks like our upstanding citizen has friends in low places."

"Show me." Tom's command bears no trace of a question as he strides forward. Cassidy obliges, pointing out transfers and accounts with the precision of an orchestral conductor.

"Money laundering?" Tom posits, piecing together the implications.

"Could be," Cassidy concedes, a tinge of pride coloring her words. "Or paying for silence... or worse."

In Tom's mind, the puzzle pieces click into place, forming a damning image of Jonathan Reynolds. The taste of justice is metallic on his tongue.

"Get your coat," he says, voice steady as bedrock, the paternal protector now donning the armor of an avenger.

✳ ✳ ✳

Tom's steps are purposeful, each one closing the distance to the man who may hold the key to unlocking the Oakwood Tragedy. Jonathan stands by the docks, the creaking boats his unwitting chorus.

"Jonathan Reynolds," Tom calls out, the name slicing the sea air.

Jonathan turns, dark eyes narrowing at the figure approaching. His lips curve into a practiced smile, but it doesn't reach those cold pools.

"Tom Blackwell, to what do I owe this intrusion?"

"Cut the act," Tom growls, his presence an immovable force against the coastal winds. "We know about your connections— your real investments."

Jonathan's facade falters, a crack in the veneer. "Accusations require proof," he retorts, defiance lacing his tone.

"Proof?" Tom counters, voice tight. "Cassidy unearthed your dirty laundry. It's only a matter of time before everything airs out."

"Allegations," Jonathan scoffs, regaining composure. "From a child playing detective? How quaint."

"Underestimate her at your peril," Tom warns, eyes locked onto his adversary. "Now, tell me about Morgan Reynolds. Tell me why her blood might be on your hands."

A moment passes, charged and heavy as storm clouds gathering over the sea. Jonathan assesses, calculates. Then, with the deliberation of a chess master contemplating a crucial move, he speaks.

"Tom, you're barking up the wrong tree. But since you're so keen on pursuing fairy tales, why not ask about the big bad wolf?"

"Save your metaphors for the jury," Tom snaps back, every word etched in the steel of conviction. "Your time's running out."

"Is that a threat?" Jonathan asks, his tone deceptively light.

"Consider it a promise," Tom replies.

They stand there, two men entangled in a deadly serious game, their shadows stretching long over the dock as the sun dips below the horizon of Oakwood.

The setting sun casts an amber glow over Oakwood's docks, where tension coils like ropes on a ship's deck. Tom stands rigid, his shadow a sharp-edged silhouette against the weathered planks. Jonathan, smooth as the calm before a storm, meets Tom's glare with practiced ease.

"Trouble in paradise, boys?" Emily's voice cuts through the stand-off, her arrival with Jack as timely as the tide. Her green eyes flick between the two men, reading the air like a seasoned sailor senses a shift in the wind.

"Emily," Tom acknowledges with a curt nod, muscles relaxing just a notch. "We were discussing some... discrepancies."

"Discrepancies?" she echoes, her tone laced with skepticism. She steps closer to Jonathan, protective in a way that sends a jolt of jealousy through Tom's veins.

"Tom thinks he's onto something," Jonathan explains, his smile disarmingly charming. "But it's all smoke and mirrors."

"Is it now?" Jack interjects, his detective's intuition pricking. "What's this about a letter, Jonathan?"

"Ah, yes." Jonathan reaches inside his jacket, producing an envelope with a theatrical flourish. "Morgan was concerned about the Leblanc kids. This should shed some light."

Tom's jaw tightens as Emily reads the letter, her brow furrowing. The words are a curveball — fear inked by Morgan's hand, casting shadows on the innocence of Clara and Charles.

"Complicating, isn't it?" Jonathan murmurs, his eyes on Emily, who remains silent, immersed in the script of doubt.

"Let's take a step back," Tom suggests, his mind racing as he steers the group away from the docks, seeking the solace of his office.

Surrounded by the fortress of files and the fortress of Nora's presence, they stand—a triad of determination. Cassidy's eyes are alight with the fire of discovery, yet clouded by the new puzzle piece.

"Didn't see that coming," Nora admits, the diner's matriarch persona giving way to the shrewdness beneath.

"Neither did I," Tom confesses, his hands splayed on the desk amidst the paper labyrinth. "We have to look at this from every angle."

Cassidy nods, already diving back into the digital depths in search of truth. "There's more to this," she insists. "Jonathan's not clean, but we need to piece it all together."

"Right." Tom's voice is gravel, his mind a stormy sea. He feels the weight of the case, heavy as the ocean's depths, and the strain on his relationship with Emily, taut as a line about to snap.

"Keep digging," he instructs, his gaze meeting Nora's steady one. "We'll unravel this knot, no matter how tangled it gets."

As they settle into their respective tasks, the night blankets Oakwood, the lighthouse beacon a solitary witness to the dance of suspicion and secrets playing out within its watchful gaze.

Emily strides into her office, the echo of her boots on the polished floor a sharp counterpoint to the cacophony of ringing phones and crackling radios. Her brow furrows as she scans the latest reports, each one a whisper of the truth, elusive and taunting.

"Mayor's on line one," Deputy Jack informs her, his voice a soft rumble in the tense air. "He's not sounding patient."

She lifts the receiver, steeling herself. "Sheriff Foster speaking."

"Emily, we need an arrest," the mayor's voice is a hammer, insistently pounding. "People are scared. They want answers, they want safety, they want it yesterday."

"An arrest without solid evidence is like a lighthouse without a bulb, useless." Emily's retort is brisk, infused with conviction. "We're close, but we're not there yet."

"Close doesn't calm the public, Em." The mayor's sigh crackles through the line, a storm brewing in the distance. "The town is a tinderbox; you know what happens if we don't contain this soon."

"Containment without cause is a bandage on a bullet wound." She leans back in her chair, the leather creaking under the burden of command. "Give me time. I'll bring you the culprit, not a scapegoat."

"Time is a luxury, Sheriff, and Oakwood's running out of it." With a click, the line goes dead, leaving Emily with the weight of a decision that could define or destroy her career.

Outside, the evening unfolds, bathed in the golden hues of fading light as the townsfolk of Oakwood continue their dance of routine and rumor, oblivious to the storm gathering behind the sheriff's steadfast gaze.

CHAPTER 8

The bell above the door chimed a nostalgic tune as Cassidy pushed through, her eyes scanning the cozy interior of the local coffee shop. Oakwood's familiar briny scent was replaced by the robust aroma of ground coffee beans and the sweet allure of pastries. With a smile tugging at her lips, she spotted Josh already there, his laptop open and an empty chair waiting beside him.

"Hey," she greeted, her voice mingling with the low hum of conversations and the occasional scrape of chairs against the floor.

"Hey, Cassie," Josh replied, his deep brown eyes lighting up. There was something about the way he said her name that made it sound like a promise of shared secrets and future adventures.

They settled into their corner nook, a space that felt a world away from the clinking cups and soft jazz drifting through the air. It was their unofficial spot, cushioned by the familiarity of worn wood and the gentle buzz of life around them. Cassidy unfurled her laptop, the screen springing to life as she turned to Josh, anticipation shimmering in her expressive blue eyes.

"Ready to dive into our applications?" she asked, her tone playful yet underscored with the seriousness of their shared goal.

"Absolutely," Josh nodded, though Cassidy noticed the tension in his jaw, a silent tell that belied his calm demeanor.

Their fingers danced across keyboards, tapping out the rhythm of two young minds on the brink of a world larger than Oakwood's quaint streets and comforting traditions. It was a dance they had grown accustomed to, a partnership formed not just in their pursuit of education, but in the trials they had weathered together.

"Look at us, huh?" Cassidy mused, her voice a soft echo of their unspoken dreams. "From building sandcastles by the docks to building futures."

"Time flies," Josh agreed, his words tinged with warmth and a trace of wistfulness. They both knew that the sands of their childhood hours had sifted through the hourglass, leaving them on the cusp of tomorrow's tide.

Around them, the coffee shop continued its gentle lull, a backdrop to the lives unfolding within its walls. The present moment was a snapshot: two laptops, two cups of coffee, two hearts beating to the drum of impending change—yet comforted by the constancy of each other's presence.

Cassidy's fingers paused mid-stroke, hovering above the keyboard as if suspended by an invisible thread of anticipation. The cursor blinked, an impatient beacon amidst a white sea of possibility. She turned her laptop to face Josh, the glow of the screen casting a soft light on her features. Her lips curled into a triumphant smile, eyes alight with a firework display of joy.

"Josh, look," she breathed out, her voice barely above a whisper, as though guarding a precious secret between them. "I got in. Harvard sent the acceptance letter."

The words cascaded into the cozy cocoon of their corner table, weaving through the steam rising from their mugs and the comforting buzz of the coffee shop. Cassidy's heart drummed a lively beat, her dream now painted in the rich crimson hues of her future alma mater.

Josh leaned forward, his gaze fixed on the bolded congratulations that adorned Cassidy's screen. His smile, genuine and proud, was a silent ovation for her achievement. Yet, as he absorbed the weight of her news, his expression shifted like an autumn leaf caught between the warmth of the sun and the chill of the breeze.

"Harvard," he echoed, allowing the word to fill the space between them. "That's incredible, Cassie. You're going to do amazing things there, especially in computer sciences."

He reached across the table, giving her hand an affirming squeeze, his touch grounding amid the flutter of excitement. The support in his tone wrapped around her like a favorite blanket, one woven from threads of shared history and mutual aspirations.

"Thanks, Josh." Cassidy's grin softened, her eyes searching his. She saw the layers of pride and concern mingled there, the complexity of emotions that often accompanied moments of change. In those deep brown pools, she read an entire novel's worth of unspoken thoughts—the resilience of his spirit tempered by the uncertainties that lay ahead.

Her focus shifted back to the screen, to the emblem of one dream realized, knowing full well that they each carried dreams of their own, parallel yet intertwined. She felt the warmth of his hand still lingering, a reminder of the bond they shared, solid and unwavering like the Oakwood lighthouse standing sentinel against the tides of time.

Cassidy's thumb paused its dance over the trackpad as she caught the way Josh's gaze drifted from her screen to the window, following a trail of leaves skittering across the sidewalk outside. The coffee shop buzzed with the energy of afternoon patrons, but in their cozy corner, the world seemed to hold its breath.

"Josh?" Cassidy leaned forward, her voice laced with concern. "What's going on inside that head of yours?"

He met her eyes, and it was like watching the tide retreat, leaving treasures and troubles alike exposed on the sand. Josh's smile was there, but it didn't reach the usual depths of his brown eyes, those windows to chapters of his life he'd often kept closed.

"Ah, I'm just..." He tapped a rhythmless beat on the table, a staccato that betrayed his inner turmoil. "I've been thinking about college, too. About Harvard."

Cassidy waited, her heart syncing to the hesitant drum of his fingers, knowing this was more than just idle thoughts. She could almost hear the cogs turning in his mind, each one hesitant to engage for fear of the machine breaking down.

"Truth is," Josh started, his voice barely above the hum of conversation around them, "I'm worried about the cost, Cassie." He exhaled, a release of more than just breath. "It's a lot. And I don't want my financial situation to be... to be something that holds you back."

In the pause that followed, Cassidy felt the weight of his confession, the heaviness of dreams threatened by the gravity of reality. She saw the pride that had kept him standing tall through storms now quivering like the sailboat masts at the docks, caught in an unforeseen gale.

"Josh," she said softly, reaching out to still his hands with her own, "you've never held me back. Not once." Her touch was meant to anchor him, to remind him that whatever currents they faced, they were in this together.

Cassidy squeezed Josh's hands, her thumbs tracing the calluses from years of football training—remnants of a past that felt both distant and endearing. She leaned in, her blue eyes locked with his, steady and unwavering. "We're a team, remember? We tackle everything head-on, together. Your dreams are just as important as mine, and we'll figure this out."

Josh's deep brown eyes flickered with the reflection of the coffee shop's warm light, revealing layers of gratitude and vulnerability. He nodded, allowing himself to be anchored by her certainty.

"Okay, so let's list our options," Cassidy suggested, her voice laced with the kind of determination that had powered countless late-night study sessions and impromptu tech repair jobs she'd done around the neighborhood.

They unfolded their laptops, the screens illuminating their faces with a soft glow, and began scouring the internet for scholarships and financial aid opportunities. Cassidy's fingers danced across the keyboard with the same agility she used to navigate complex coding problems.

"Look at this," she said, pointing to a scholarship for students interested in STEM fields. "This could be a start. And there's got to be something for you too. You've got a way with words that could charm the staunchest grant committee."

"Maybe," Josh allowed, his tone still carrying a thread of doubt. But Cassidy's optimism was infectious; it filled the gaps between them, weaving a safety net beneath their high-flying aspirations.

"And if we have to," Cassidy continued, her gaze now drifting beyond the laptop screen to the bustling life of Oakwood outside, "we can find part-time jobs. I hear Nora's Diner might need extra help, especially since they stay open later now."

"Balancing jobs and Harvard coursework?" Josh asked, arching an eyebrow but with a smile tugging at his lips.

"Hey, we thrive under pressure, right?" Cassidy replied, her own smile reflecting the playful challenge. "Besides, we can study on shift breaks. Multitasking is my middle name."

"Mine's 'try not to trip over air while multitasking,'" Josh quipped, earning a burst of laughter from Cassidy that melted into the surrounding symphony of clinking cups and murmured conversations.

"Then it's settled. We apply for every piece of financial aid we can get our hands on, and we make a backup plan for work. We'll manage. We always do." Her words weren't just hopeful; they were a prophecy of their shared future, cast with the conviction that only youthful love and combined resolve could muster.

Josh squeezed her hand in return, the gesture simple yet laden with shared purpose. They were two threads spun from the same fabric of Oakwood, intertwined with the strength of family bonds and the resilience shaped by personal trials.

"Team Cassidy and Josh," he said, a declaration more than a statement.

"You know it," Cassidy affirmed, her heart swelling with the familiar warmth of tradition, the comforting weight of time spent and yet to come, all converging in the quaint haven of their seaside town. Together, they turned back to their screens, their minds buzzing with strategies and their spirits buoyed by the unshakeable belief in each other.

Josh tapped his fingers against the worn wood of the corner table, a rhythmless drumming that betrayed his inner turmoil. The screen before him glowed with the Harvard crest, a beacon of dreams just out of reach. Cassidy's laptop, open beside his, displayed a similar page, but hers was adorned with the thrilling addition of an acceptance letter.

"Hey," Cassidy said gently, her voice pulling Josh back from the precipice of his worries. "You remember Mrs. Hawthorne's reaction when you submitted that essay on 'The Great Gatsby'? She practically gushed about it for a week straight."

Josh gave a half-hearted smile, the memory a small comfort. "Yeah, she did say something about Fitzgerald rolling in his grave with envy."

"Exactly!" Cassidy's eyes sparkled like the ocean waves catching the last of the day's light. "There are scholarships for that kind of talent, you know. Writing scholarships. You should apply."

A writing scholarship. The idea hovered in the air between them, tangible as the aroma of roasted coffee beans and just as rich with possibility. Josh's gaze flicked to Cassidy, then away, a tide of doubt pulling at him.

"Come on, those things are for prodigies or people with connections," he said, his words carrying the weight of a truth he had come to accept.

Cassidy leaned forward, her expression earnest and fierce. "But you are a prodigy, in your own right. Your passion for literature, the way you write—it's remarkable, Josh." Her hand reached across the table, fingers brushing against his. "I believe in you. And, I think it's time you start doing the same."

Her belief was a lifeline, strong and unyielding. It was the kind of support that felt like home—like Oakwood itself, with its enduring lighthouse standing guard, its friendly faces, and the timeless traditions that stitched the fabric of the community together. In Cassidy's unwavering gaze, Josh found a reflection of the strength that had carried him through the darkest of times.

"Okay," he finally breathed out, the word feeling like a door opening to a path he hadn't dared to tread. "I'll give it a shot."

"Good." Cassidy's smile was triumphant, a shared victory in the making. "We'll find the right one, and we'll work on it together. Just like everything else."

In that cozy corner of the coffee shop, amidst the backdrop of familiar noises and the soft, golden hues of the setting sun streaming through the windows, Josh felt a warmth envelop him. It wasn't just the promise of future success; it was the realization that, no matter the outcome, they would face it as a team.

"Thank you, Cass," he said, his gratitude as deep as the roots of the old oaks lining the streets outside. "For believing in me."

Cassidy reached across the table and tapped Josh's laptop with a deliberate finger, her eyes dancing with resolve. "Alright, so let's set aside time twice a week. Tuesdays and Thursdays work for you?" Her voice was as rhythmic as the waves that lapped at Oakwood's shores.

"Sounds perfect," Josh agreed, his tone taking on a buoyancy that had been absent just moments before. He clicked open a new document, the blank page staring back at them like a challenge to be met head-on.

"First things first, we brainstorm," Cassidy declared, her mind already racing with potential themes and anecdotes that Josh could weave into his essay. "Your passion for literature is a given, but we need something that grabs them, something personal but universal. Remember how you compared life in Oakwood to a Steinbeck novel?"

Josh chuckled, a sound that mingled pleasantly with the light clinks of coffee cups around them. "Yeah, I might have gotten a bit carried away with that one."

"Carried away is good; it shows you care." Cassidy leaned in closer, her presence an embodiment of encouragement. "We can meet here after track practice, and we'll make sure your essay reflects exactly who you are. Not just the former quarterback or the guy dealing with...everything," she said, her words tiptoeing around the tragedy that shadowed his past.

"Thanks, Cassie." Josh's smile was genuine, a testament to the trust he placed in her hands. They mapped out their schedule, penciling in sessions amidst schoolwork and extracurriculars, turning Cassidy's planner into a tapestry of plans and possibilities.

As the sun dipped lower, casting an amber glow over the coffee shop, they began to pack up their laptops and notes. The world outside the window transitioned into twilight, painting the town in shades of nostalgia that only Oakwood's autumn could bring.

"Hey," Cassidy said softly, halting Josh's movements. She reached out, her hand finding his, their fingers intertwining with ease. "No matter what happens, we're in this together. Okay?" Her eyes held a promise, as steady as the old lighthouse that stood watch over their coastal haven.

Josh felt the weight of her words settle within him, a comforting anchor amidst the tides of uncertainty. "Together," he echoed in his head, squeezing her hand, feeling the strength that flowed from her resolve into his own doubts, fortifying them.

In that small act of connection, they found more than shared goals; they found a shared spirit, the kind that had seen generations of Oakwood residents through both trials and triumphs. As they stood, their hands still clasped, there was a silent agreement that whatever their future held, it would be faced side by side.

"Let's do this, partner," Cassidy said with a playful wink, her sassy edge making a brief appearance.

"Lead the way, Blackwell," Josh replied, his use of her last name a nod to their unspoken pact.

They gathered their belongings, leaving behind the echo of their laughter and the warmth of a corner table that had witnessed the beginning of a journey—a journey not just toward college, but toward a dream they dared to chase together.

Cassidy pushed open the door of the coffee shop, a gentle bell chiming above them as they stepped out into the embrace of Oakwood's quaint streets. The afternoon was yielding to evening, and the sun's golden hue bathed the town in a serene glow that seemed to echo their hopeful sentiments.

Josh let the door swing shut behind them, his gaze fixed on the horizon where the iconic lighthouse stood sentinel against the deepening sky. Its steadfast beam reminded him of Cassidy's support, a beacon guiding him through his doubts.

"Can you smell that?" Cassidy inhaled deeply, her eyes closing for a moment as the scent of the ocean mingled with the earthy fragrance of fallen leaves. "It's like every autumn, Oakwood wraps itself in a cloak."

"Yeah," Josh agreed, taking a lungful of the crisp air himself. "It's like time slows down here, makes you appreciate the little things." He watched as a swirl of amber and crimson leaves danced across their path, propelled by a playful gust of wind.

They walked shoulder to shoulder, the rhythm of their steps syncing with the quiet cadence of the town as if they were part of its heartbeat. Cassidy pointed to a maple tree, its branches a cascade of fiery hues. "I'm going to miss this when we're at Harvard. The way Oakwood just...shows off in the fall."

"We'll come back for it," Josh said, certainty firm in his voice. "Thanksgiving breaks, long weekends... We won't just abandon this place."

"Promise?" Cassidy looked at him, her blue eyes reflecting the twilight.

"Promise," he nodded, feeling the weight of tradition and the comforting cycle of seasons that had marked his life in Oakwood.

Their conversation meandered like the winding cobblestone

paths beneath their feet, touching on professors they hoped to learn from, dorms they wished to live in, and the adventures that awaited them in lecture halls and libraries.

"Imagine us, cramming for finals together or debating over code and Chaucer," Cassidy mused, a laugh escaping her lips.

"Hey, maybe we'll solve some real-life mysteries too," Josh quipped, playing along with the whimsy of their dreams. "Oakwood Tragedy part two?"

"Only if it ends with us cracking the case," she shot back playfully, nudging him with her elbow.

As the daylight dwindled, storefronts began to flicker to life, their warm glows inviting the evening crowd. They passed Nora's Diner, where the aroma of dinner service teased their senses, promising comfort in every savory note.

"Remember when we used to press our faces against the glass, trying to guess what Nora was cooking?" Cassidy asked, a smile curving her lips at the memory.

"Hard to forget. You always guessed right," Josh admitted, his admiration for her keen perception never waning.

"Guess it runs in the family," she said, thinking of Emily, her father's fiancée and the sharp-shooting sheriff—a woman whose instincts were as finely tuned as her wit.

"Must be nice," Josh chuckled, though he knew his own strengths lay elsewhere, in words and stories.

"Let's head to the pier," Cassidy suggested, pointing toward the water. "One last look before we go home?"

"Lead the way," Josh replied, content to follow her into the evening's embrace.

Together, they navigated the familiar route, their thoughts twined with shared aspirations and the unspoken knowledge that wherever life took them, the heart of Oakwood would always be their anchor.

The pier stretched out before them, a wooden finger pointing toward the horizon where the sun had surrendered to the twilight. Cassidy, her steps in rhythm with the creaking planks beneath their feet, leaned into Josh's side, her head resting on his shoulder as if it were the most natural perch in the world.

"Remember when we thought this old pier was endless?" she murmured, her voice tinged with the kind of nostalgia that painted even the mundane with magic. "Like if we ran fast enough, we'd fly right off into the sky."

Josh smiled, his arm slipping around her waist. "Feels like yesterday and a lifetime ago," he said, his words a soft exhale in the cooling air. The scent of saltwater mingled with the earthiness of damp wood, a blend as familiar as the freckles dusting Cassidy's nose—each one a constellation he'd memorized over countless summers spent by her side.

They paused at the end of the pier, where the world opened up, offering them an expanse of water that glimmered with the last vestiges of day. Cassidy's eyes, blue as the ocean they gazed upon, shone with the reflection of their shared dreams—a future at Harvard, challenges met hand in hand, victories celebrated in each other's embrace.

"Look at us," she said, her laugh a cascade of warmth in the chill evening, "planning our escape since we were kids, and now we're actually doing it."

"Doesn't feel real, does it?" Josh replied. His doubts and fears had dissolved in the face of Cassidy's unwavering support—their bond a testament to resilience, to the enduring love that had taken root in the fertile soil of friendship and blossomed amidst adversity.

"Hey," Cassidy turned to him, her fingers gently lifting his chin, ensuring their eyes met. "Wherever we go, whatever happens, we've got this. We've always been a pretty good team."

"Best team," Josh corrected, a smile playing on his lips as he wrapped her in an embrace that felt like coming home. They stood there, holding each other, two young hearts beating against the backdrop of the lapping waves and the distant call of seagulls bidding the day goodbye.

"Promise me something?" Cassidy whispered, her breath warm against his neck.

"Anything," he promised back.

"Promise we'll never forget this place. Our little seaside haven."

"Oakwood's part of us," he assured her, his voice steady and true.

"Can't forget it any more than I could forget you."

With a sigh of contentment, Cassidy nestled closer, her arms tightening around him. They lingered there, suspended between the promise of tomorrow and the sweet sorrow of leaving behind the town that had cradled their childhood.

As the stars began to prick holes in the darkening sky, they finally pulled away, hands still clasped, their gazes locked in a silent vow. And in that moment, time seemed to bow in reverence to their journey—a journey not measured in distance, but in the depth of connection that would carry them forward, together, toward a dream as vast as the sea itself.

"Let's make it an adventure," Cassidy said with a grin that set Josh's heart alight.

"Always," he agreed, and with one last look at the tapestry of Oakwood's twilight, they turned from the pier and walked back through the town that had raised them, their steps light with hope and the boundless certainty of youth.

CHAPTER 9

Emily's boots clicked along the weathered floorboards of the Blackwell's front porch as she approached the carved oak door. She lifted the brass knocker, its metallic rap echoing through the still morning air. Her fingers absently traced the familiar contours - how many times had she announced her arrival on this very porch over the years?

The door swung open to reveal Cassidy's slender frame, clad in an oversized Harvard sweatshirt. Emily's lips curved into a smile. "Hey kiddo, got time for a chat?"

Cassidy's eyes narrowed almost imperceptibly. "Sure Em, c'mon in."

Emily stepped across the threshold, memories washing over her - late nights curled up on the sofa watching old movies, the rich aroma of Tom's famous pancakes on weekend mornings, raucous family game nights filled with laughter.

Cassidy led the way to the living room, its furnishings bearing witness to generations of Blackwell traditions. Emily settled into the worn leather armchair she knew so well, Cassidy perching on the sofa across from her. Silence hung in the air.

"So..." Emily began, "I wanted to check in, see how you're holding up. I know things have been tough lately, with the investigation and all. You know you can always talk to me, right?"

Cassidy nodded, eyes fixed on Emily's phone resting on the side table. Emily followed her gaze.

"Expecting a call?" Cassidy asked, her voice taut.

"No, just didn't want any distractions. Like I said, I'm here for you..."

Cassidy lunged forward, snatching the phone. Her thumbs flew as she scanned the screen. Emily froze.

"What the hell is this?" Cassidy demanded, eyes ablaze.

Emily's heart sank. The text - the one confirming the accomplice's murder. Her secret was out.

"Cass, I can explain..." she started weakly.

"Explain??" Cassidy cried. "You've been hiding things from us, from Dad! How could you??"

Emily took a deep breath, pulse racing. "I was trying to protect you both. Please, let me explain..."

The words tumbled out as Emily revealed the truth. Cassidy listened, anger mingling with hurt as the tale unfolded.

When Emily finished, Cassidy shook her head slowly. "I don't know what to believe anymore. I thought we trusted each other."

Emily reached out a hand, voice thick with emotion. "We do sweetheart. I never meant to hurt you. I just didn't know what to do..."

Cassidy turned away, the gulf between them suddenly vast. Emily's heart fractured, knowing that only time could mend the bonds she had broken.

Cassidy paced the room, arms crossed tightly across her chest. Her eyes glistened with tears she refused to shed.

"How could you keep this from us?" she demanded. "From me?"

Emily stood helplessly. "Cassidy, I—"

"Don't!" Cassidy snapped. "Just don't. I thought you cared about this family. But it's clear your job takes priority."

"That's not fair," Emily pleaded. "I was trying to protect you both."

"Protect us?" Cassidy retorted. "Or protect yourself?"

Emily flinched at the accusation. Before she could respond, the door flew open. Tom strode in, his brow knitted in concern.

"What's going on here?"

Cassidy whirled to face him, fresh tears spilling down her cheeks.

"Dad, Emily's been keeping things from us about the case to protect herself."

Tom looked stunned. He turned to Emily.

"Emily...is this true?"

Emily opened her mouth but no words emerged. Tom's eyes darkened with disappointment.

"I trusted you," he said quietly. "We both did."

Cassidy buried her face in Tom's shoulder. He wrapped a protective arm around her, his expression pained.

Emily's voice shook. "Tom, please, let me explain..."

But Tom just shook his head sadly.

"I think you've done enough explaining for today."

Defeated, Emily turned and walked out, the damage she had caused trailing behind her like a fractured seam she could never mend.

Emily retreated to the sanctuary of her patrol car, its familiarity offering little comfort. Collapsing into the driver's seat, she finally allowed the tears to fall. They streamed down her cheeks, cutting a path through the foundation she carefully applied each morning before duty called.

With shaking hands, she reached for the visor and flipped open the mirror. A broken woman stared back at her. The strong, confident sheriff was gone, replaced by someone Emily barely recognized.

She thought back to that fateful morning at the academy when she first pinned on her badge, swelling with pride and purpose. She had sworn an oath to protect and serve, no matter the cost.

Somewhere along the way, the lines blurred. Her ambition clouded her judgment, ambition born from having to prove herself in a man's world. She clawed her way up the ranks, refusing to be defined by outdated gender roles.

But now, kneeling at the altar of her own ego, the price was clear. She had sacrificed the very relationships she had fought so hard to build, all for the sake of control and self-preservation.

A sharp rap at the window startled her from her thoughts. She looked up to see Tom peering in, his eyes unreadable. Wiping her tears, she stepped out to face him.

"We need to talk," he said gruffly, motioning for her to follow him.

In silence they walked, past the lighthouse and onto the rocky shore. The cold sea air stung Emily's cheeks. Finally, Tom stopped, gazing out at the slate-grey waves.

"Why didn't you come to me?" he asked without turning. "I could've helped you."

Emily hugged herself against the chill. "It wasn't that simple. You're defending the suspects."

Tom shook his head. "My role doesn't change the fact that I care about you. About us."

He paused, struggling to find the words. Emily remained quiet, sensing there was more he needed to say.

"I remember how eager you were to join the force," he continued. "You had such conviction. Such spirit. It's what drew me to you."

He turned to face her. "So what happened, Emily? When did the job become more important than the people you serve? Than your own family?"

His words pierced her heart. Fresh tears spilled down her cheeks.

"I don't know," she whispered.

Tom stepped closer, his eyes glistening. "I think you do. Deep down, you know."

Emily's breath caught in her throat. She saw the truth reflecting back at her in Tom's eyes.

This was never about the job. It was about her need for control, her fear of being vulnerable. If she kept others at arm's length, they couldn't hurt her.

But in doing so, she had hurt them instead.

"I'm so sorry," she choked out. "You're absolutely right."

She took Tom's hand, pouring all her regret and love into that simple gesture.

"I know we have a long road ahead," she said softly. "But I'm ready to do the work. However long it takes."

For the first time, Tom squeezed her hand back. The tide was turning.

Emily took a deep, steadying breath and began to open up.

"When I first joined the force, I was so idealistic," she said quietly. "I thought I could single-handedly take down the bad guys and keep everyone safe."

She gave a rueful laugh. "Pretty naïve, huh?"

Tom's expression softened. "We all start out that way. Full of dreams and good intentions."

Emily nodded, a faraway look in her eyes. "But this job...it changes you. The things I've seen..." She trailed off, shaking her head.

"You start to build up walls. Become guarded. I've just seen so much pain and loss over the years. I couldn't bear the thought of letting anyone in, only to lose them too."

She turned to Cassidy, unshed tears glistening. "Especially you, sweetheart. I know I've made mistakes, but everything I did was to try and protect my family."

Cassidy blinked rapidly, fighting back her own tears.

"I understand that now," she said, her voice thick with emotion. "I'm sorry I got so angry. I was just...scared."

"We all were," Tom said gently. He put a hand on Cassidy's shoulder. "But the truth is, we're strongest together. It's time for the secrets to end."

Cassidy rushed forward and threw her arms around Emily.

"I've missed you so much," she whispered.

Emily clung to her tightly, the dam finally breaking as tears of relief streamed down her face.

"I promise, no more lies," she murmured. "I don't want to lose this family."

They stayed locked in an embrace, the air cleansed by honesty and forgiveness. There would still be challenges ahead, but they would face them together.

Tom let out a heavy sigh, the emotional weight of the confrontation settling over him. Though progress had been made, there was still tension lingering in the room.

"I think we could all use some time to process this," he said wearily, running a hand through his disheveled hair. "It's been...a lot."

Emily pulled back from Cassidy and nodded, wiping the remnants of tears from her eyes.

"You're right," she agreed, her voice raspy. "We shouldn't try to fix everything tonight."

She turned to Cassidy, who gave her a small, reassuring smile. There was still hurt there, but the anger had dissipated.

"I know I have a lot more to explain," Emily said. "Whenever you're ready to talk again, I'll be here."

Cassidy nodded, the hint of a smirk playing at her lips. "Don't think you're off the hook yet. We've still got plenty to discuss."

The subtle return of Cassidy's humor lifted the mood, giving them all a glimmer of hope. There was still a long road ahead, but the air felt clearer now.

Tom walked over and put an arm around Cassidy's shoulders. "Come on, let's give Emily some space. I'll make us some tea."

Cassidy leaned into her father's embrace, some of the tension leaving her body. As they started to walk away, she glanced over her shoulder.

"Emily...thank you. For being honest. It means a lot."

Emily's eyes glistened again. "Of course. Get some rest, both of you. I'll come by tomorrow so we can talk more."

Tom and Cassidy made their way to the kitchen, the weight of the day showing in their weary footsteps. Emily let out a shaky breath, emotionally spent. It would take time to rebuild the broken trust, but for the first time in weeks, she felt a sense of hope about the future.

The setting sun cast an amber glow across the living room as Josh approached Cassidy, who was sitting alone on the couch staring vacantly out the window. She barely registered his presence as he sat down beside her.

"Hey," he said softly. "That was...intense. Are you doing okay?"

Cassidy let out a long sigh, her eyes never leaving the horizon. "Honestly? I have no idea how I'm feeling right now. It's like my emotions have been put in a blender."

She turned to Josh, traces of hurt still lingering on her face. "I just can't believe Emily would keep something like that from us.

From me. I thought we trusted each other."

Josh nodded in understanding. "I know. It sucks when someone you care about betrays that trust." He hesitated before continuing gently, "But maybe try to see it from her perspective too? She was in an impossible position."

Cassidy furrowed her brow. "Whose side are you on anyway?" she snapped.

Josh held up his hands defensively. "Hey, I'm on your side, always. I just think the situation was more complicated than it seems."

Cassidy's features softened. "You're right, I shouldn't take this out on you. It's just...everything feels like it's changing so fast. I got accepted to Harvard, but the thought of leaving Oakwood..." Her voice trailed off.

"Yeah, about that..." Josh shifted, his discomfort apparent. "Have you thought more about what happens after graduation? For us, I mean?"

Cassidy looked at him quizzically. "What do you mean? I'll be in Boston, you'll be coming too, but we'll make it work."

Josh stood up abruptly and paced in front of her. "That's just it though, you have it all figured out. But I still have no idea what I'm doing next year. Everyone assumes I'm leaving too, but I don't any offers yet. I feel so lost."

Cassidy's eyes widened in surprise. "Josh, why didn't you tell me you were feeling this way?"

He turned to her, vulnerability etched on his face. "I don't know. I guess I didn't want to let you down. Or hold you back."

"You could never let me down." Cassidy grabbed his hand, forcing him to look at her. "Listen to me. I told you we'll figure your future out together. I'm not going anywhere."

Josh managed a small smile, the reassurance momentarily easing his worries. There were still uncertainties ahead, but Cassidy's steadfast loyalty was his port in the storm.

CHAPTER 10

E mily sat at her desk, staring absently out the window as
dusk settled over Oakwood. The last rays of sunlight
glinted off the swaying masts in the harbor, but Emily's
gaze was turned inward. Her mind churned with the new
evidence that had surfaced in the Reynolds case, overturning
her initial theory. She had been so certain Jonathan was
involved, but now...Emily sighed, leaning back in her chair.
There was more to this than she realized.

She thought of Tom and felt a pang of regret. She had pushed
him away, convinced of her own flawed suspicions. Emily
pictured his kind eyes and steady presence, wishing he was here
to help make sense of it all. She missed his wry humor and the
way he always listened before offering his insights.

Determined to make things right, Emily reached for the phone
on her desk, her heart quickening. She dialed the familiar
number, gripping the receiver tightly as it rang.

"Hello?" Tom's low voice greeted her.

"Tom, it's Emily," she began tentatively. "I know it's been a while, but I wanted to talk to you about the case."

"Oh?" Tom responded. Emily heard the surprise in his tone.

"I was wrong to shut you out. I realize that now. There are pieces that aren't adding up and I could really use your help." Emily spoke earnestly, hoping Tom could hear the sincerity in her words.

There was a pause before Tom replied gently, "I appreciate you calling, Em. I'm happy to look everything over again with fresh eyes."

Emily exhaled in relief, a small smile touching her lips. "Thank you, Tom. That means a lot. I've missed working with you."

"Likewise," Tom said warmly. "Why don't you swing by my office first thing tomorrow? We'll get to the bottom of this, together."

"It's a date," Emily affirmed. As she set down the phone, she felt the burden on her shoulders lift. With Tom by her side once more, she was confident they would uncover the truth.

Emily arrived at Tom's office early the next morning, a stack of case files tucked under her arm. She was greeted by the familiar organized chaos - stacks of legal books and mountains of paperwork strewn across every surface.

Tom looked up from his desk as she entered, rising to give her a quick hug.

"It's good to see you, Em," he said sincerely. Emily smiled, the lingering awkwardness between them dissipating.

They sat across from each other and Emily began laying out the various documents, crime scene photos, and interview transcripts.

"I keep coming back to the neighbor's statement about seeing a dark sedan near the house that night," Emily said, shuffling through papers. "It doesn't line up with Morgan's car or anyone else's in the family."

Tom nodded thoughtfully, jotting down notes. "We should track down that lead. Maybe canvas the neighborhood again, see if anyone else noticed an unfamiliar vehicle."

The hours passed quickly as they analyzed evidence, bouncing theories back and forth. Emily felt a familiar rhythm settling between them, their conversation interspersed with comfortable silences.

"You know, I think we need to take a closer look at Morgan's ex-husband," Tom eventually remarked. "There's definitely bad blood there that bears further investigation."

Emily met his gaze, feeling energized by their progress. With Tom's insight, this complex web was starting to unravel. There was still much work to be done, but she was confident that together, they would bring clarity to this tragedy.

Emily's eyes lit up as she processed Tom's suggestion. "Jonathan

Reynolds...JR Holdings...I can't believe I didn't make that connection before."

She rifled through the papers, pulling out a copy of Morgan and Jonathan's divorce settlement. "It looks like it was a messy split - they went through a lengthy court battle over the house and he still owed Morgan money for his business, JR Holdings, he was starting at the time that failed."

Tom leaned in, intrigued. "So Jonathan had motive and opportunity. This is a solid lead, Em."

Emily nodded, feeling a swell of excitement. "Let's bring him in for questioning. I have a feeling he knows more than he's letting on."

Tom smiled, a familiar glint in his eye. "Just like old times, partner."

Emily laughed. "Some things never change. C'mon, let's go rattle his cage a bit." She paused, meeting Tom's gaze. "I'm glad we're in this together."

Tom squeezed her shoulder warmly. "Me too. We make a good team."

With renewed determination, they gathered their things. The truth was within reach, Emily could feel it. And with Tom by her side, she knew they would uncover it.

* * *

Cassidy set a tall glass of iced tea in front of Josh and took a seat across from him at the worn kitchen table.

"Alright, let's get this essay written," she said, giving him an encouraging smile. "I know you've got some great ideas in that head of yours."

Josh stared down at the blank paper, clicking his pen absently. "I don't know...my thoughts are all jumbled. I can't seem to get the words out."

Cassidy reached over and put a hand on his arm. "Hey, it's okay. We'll figure this out together."

She thought for a moment. "Why don't we start with the prompt? Remind me what they're looking for."

"They want a personal essay about an experience that shaped who I am," Josh sighed.

Cassidy's eyes lit up. "Well that's perfect! You have so many amazing experiences to draw from. Let's brainstorm."

She grabbed a notebook and started jotting down ideas as Josh spoke. He slowly opened up, sharing meaningful memories from his childhood on the farm, summers spent fishing with his grandpa, and the thrills and challenges of playing football. Then there was the devastation of his mother's murder and his father's arrest.

Cassidy listened intently, asking thoughtful questions. As Josh recalled a particular fishing trip, his eyes grew misty. Cassidy squeezed his hand gently.

"That sounds like a great focus for your essay. You could write about how that trip taught you patience and perseverance."

Josh nodded, a faint smile crossing his face. "Yeah...you're right. That could work. Plus its one of my few happy family memories"

Cassidy grinned. "See? I knew you had it in you! Now let's get these memories into words. I'll help you polish it up after the first draft."

With Cassidy's encouragement, the words began to flow...

* * *

The air was thick with tension as Emily and Tom stood across from Jonathan in the plush living room of his seaside home. Though his smile was relaxed, his eyes held a frantic glint that gave away his unraveling composure.

"To what do I owe the pleasure of this visit?" Jonathan purred, his tone dripping with forced charm.

Emily's gaze was steely. "I think you know why we're here. We have evidence that links you to Morgan Reynolds' murder."

Jonathan's smile faded, but he quickly recovered. "Now Emily, let's not jump to conclusions. I know tensions are high after that poor woman's death, but I had nothing to do with it."

Tom crossed his arms. "We have phone records showing you called Morgan multiple times leading up to the night she died. Care to explain that?"

Sweat beaded on Jonathan's forehead. "I was simply checking on the children. You know I care deeply for their wellbeing."

"So deeply that Clara witnessed you threatening Morgan the week before her murder?" Emily challenged.

Jonathan paled. For a moment, his polished veneer cracked, revealing a hint of desperation. But he quickly composed himself.

"The girl is clearly confused. I never made any such threats."

Tom slammed his hand on the coffee table, causing Jonathan to flinch.

"Enough lies! We know about the money you owed Morgan. Admit what you did so we can end this!"

Jonathan jumped to his feet, all pretense gone.

"You have nothing on me!" he shouted. "I won't let you destroy everything I've built!"

Emily shook her head. "It's over, Jonathan. The evidence doesn't lie."

"If you had more then circumstantial evidence, you'd be here to arrest me Sheriff, not make accusations," said Jonthan in a smug tone." I think you guy's have spent too much time in this fishing town, because thats all you're doing."

After that he got up showed Tom and Emily the door.

Emily and Tom exchanged a look of relief and triumph. At last, they knew he was their man and justice will be served.

As they turned away and went back to the Blackwell residence, Emily turned to Tom on the porch, placing a gentle hand on his arm. "I can't thank you enough for everything you've done. If it wasn't for you, I would never have looked at this case differently."

Tom gave her a small smile. "You don't need to thank me. Solving this case together was the right thing to do."

"It was more than that," Emily said earnestly. "You inspired me to see the truth when I was blinded by my own assumptions. And you opened my heart again when I thought it was closed forever."

She stepped closer, her green eyes glistening. "I know we have a complicated history, but throughout this journey, I've realized what matters most. You're the one I want by my side, today and always."

Tom's stoic facade softened. He took Emily's hands in his own. "After losing your mother, I never imagined I could feel this way again. But you've given me hope for the future. Hope that we can build a life together, with trust, understanding and love."

Emily smiled radiantly. "Then let's stop living in the past. When this is all over, will you marry me and see where this new journey takes us?"

Tom pulled her into an embrace. "Nothing would make me happier. Our future begins today."

They held each other close, two kindred souls reunited at long last. The mystery had broken down the walls between them, revealing a lasting bond ready to blossom anew.

Emily and Tom stayed locked in a tender embrace, taking comfort in the promise of their future together. Nearby, Cassidy smiled knowingly as she watched the two of them, happy to see her father finally open his heart again.

Beside Cassidy, Josh let out a contented sigh. "Well, I think our work here is done," he said with a grin. "Your dad and Emily look pretty happy."

Cassidy nudged him playfully. "Yeah, we make a good team, don't we?" She paused, her expression growing serious. "Listen, Josh...I'm really glad we could work things out between us. I know it hasn't been easy, but you mean so much to me."

Josh took her hand, his eyes full of warmth. "You mean everything to me too, Cass. All I want is to see you succeed and be happy. Speaking of which..." He nodded towards the thick envelope sitting on the table.

Cassidy's face lit up. It was the acceptance letter from Harvard, her dream school. "I still can't believe I got in," she said. "But I couldn't have done it without you."

She threw her arms around Josh in an enthusiastic hug. He laughed and hugged her back. "Hey, you got yourself in with all your hard work. But I'm happy I could help."

As they parted, Cassidy met his eyes resolutely. "And now I'm going to return the favor. We're going to get your writing scholarship essay done tonight." She grabbed his hand and pulled him towards the desk.

Josh took a seat as Cassidy rifled through her drawers for pens and paper. Her passion and determination ignited his own excitement to pursue this dream. With Cassidy's help, he knew anything was possible.

The future shone bright with promise - new adventures, new dreams, and new beginnings. But most of all, it held the hope of lasting love.

CHAPTER 11

The setting sun cast an ominous glow over the ramshackle bar's cracked windows as Tom cut the engine outside The Crow's Nest. He and Emily exchanged a knowing glance, mentally preparing for the task ahead.

Tom stepped out of the car, the salty sea air prickling his skin. This was the seediest part of Oakwood, and The Crow's Nest had a reputation as a den of thieves and lowlifes. But if their tip was correct, the witness they sought knew these shadows better than anyone.

Emily emerged beside Tom, her emerald eyes scanning the street. He couldn't help but admire how the fading light illuminated her auburn hair. Focus, he reminded himself, though her beauty still stirred something in him, even after all these years.

They approached the bar entrance cautiously, the muffled sound of rowdy laughter leaking out into the night. Tom's hand instinctively checked for the revolver tucked in his waistband. Emily nodded, ready.

Pushing the door open released a wave of sour booze,

tobacco smoke, and unwashed bodies. Raucous patrons crowded mismatched tables while a hulking bartender manned the counter.

Tom spotted their contact immediately. Jake's imposing frame didn't quite match the warm crinkle of his eyes as he greeted them.

"Jake Jurisky?" Tom kept his tone hushed amidst the chaos. Jake gave a nearly imperceptible nod in return.

"We need to talk, privately." Emily's voice was steady but firm.

Jake glanced around before beckoning them toward a back storeroom. Sheltered from prying eyes, he spoke in a gravelly whisper. "I'll tell you what I know about the night Morgan Reynolds was murdered. But we don't have much time."

Jake's eyes darted nervously toward the storeroom door as he began.

"I was working that night like usual. Around 10pm, I noticed a shifty character slip in and sit alone in the corner booth. He ordered a few drinks, but mostly kept to himself."

Jake paused, brow furrowed as if debating how much to reveal. Tom and Emily exchanged a look but remained silent, letting Jake take his time.

"An hour later, two more men entered. They joined the first guy in the booth and I saw them exchanging money and documents.

Couldn't hear what they were saying over the noise."

He hesitated again before continuing, his voice barely above a whisper. "But I did catch two names. Morgan Reynolds and..."

Suddenly, the storeroom door burst open. Three men stormed in, shoving Jake against the wall. Tom and Emily scrambled back, hands reaching for their weapons.

"Well well, what do we have here?" the largest man leered. He turned to Tom and Emily. "I think it's time for you two to leave. Wouldn't want this to get...messy."

Tom stepped forward, jaw set. "We're not going anywhere until we get the information we need." Emily flanked him, eyes blazing.

The thug laughed coldly. "Big mistake." He lunged toward Tom.

Emily's revolver was in her hand in an instant. "I wouldn't do that if I were you," she warned. The men froze as she cocked the hammer back with an audible click.

A tense beat passed. Then the leader nodded and the men slowly backed out of the storeroom.

Tom let out a breath. "Thanks for the save."

Emily smiled tightly. "Anytime, partner." She turned to Jake. "Now, where were we?"

Jake's eyes darted between Tom and Emily, still on edge from the confrontation.

"Like I said, I heard two names that night - Morgan Reynolds and..."

His words were drowned out by a sudden commotion from the bar. Shouting voices escalated into the unmistakable sounds of a brawl. Glass shattered, tables overturned.

Tom and Emily exchanged a glance. This was their chance to slip away unnoticed.

"We need to go, now," Tom said. He clasped Jake's shoulder. "Thank you, my friend. We'll be in touch."

Jake nodded, his kind eyes conveying a wordless message - be careful.

Emily peered out the storeroom door. "Coast is clear, let's move."

They hurried through the chaos engulfing the bar, weaving between brawling patrons until they reached the exit. The cool night air was a stark contrast to the heat of the bar fight they left behind.

Once outside, Tom let out a long exhale. "That was close. We need to regroup and figure out our next step."

Emily nodded, leading them around the corner into the alley.

Her brows furrowed in thought.

"Jake was about to give us a solid lead until those goons showed up. Whoever he named, they want to keep it quiet." She met Tom's eyes. "I think it's time we pay the mayor a visit."

Tom frowned. "You think Mayor Elliot is involved somehow?"

"It's just a hunch, but he's been too quiet lately, too removed from the investigation. And he had close ties with Morgan Reynolds." Emily clenched her jaw. "I say we search his office, see if we can find anything linking him to this."

Tom considered this, then nodded. "Alright, let's do it. But we'll have to be smart - the mayor is sure to have security."

Emily smirked. "Then it's a good thing we make a great team."

She checked her revolver and straightened her badge. Side by side, she and Tom strode into the night, heading straight for the viper's nest.

Tom and Emily approached the mayor's office, a stately brick building in the heart of downtown. Though it was late, a few lights still glowed in the windows.

"There's a side entrance that's usually unmanned this time of night," Emily murmured. "We can slip in that way."

They crept through the shadows and reached the door. Emily pulled out her lockpick set and had the door open in seconds.

After checking that the coast was clear, they slipped inside.

The office was dark and silent. Moonlight filtering through the blinds cast barred shadows across the plush carpet. They moved carefully between desks and file cabinets, heading for the mayor's personal office in the back.

Emily tried the handle - locked. Kneeling, she once again worked her magic.

As the door swung open, Tom tensed. The spacious office felt cavernous in the dark. He swept his flashlight around, pausing on the large mahogany desk.

"Let's start there," he whispered.

They began opening drawers and rifling through files. Most contained mundane documents - schedules, memos, invoices. Nothing about Morgan Reynolds or the murder case.

Frustrated, Tom sat back. His flashlight glinted off something - a small gap along the desk's side. Curious, he ran his fingers along it.

"A hidden compartment," he murmured. He pressed along the edge until it popped open. Inside lay a stack of manila folders. Pulling one out, Tom saw the name: Reynolds.

"Jackpot," he breathed. Emily crossed over to look just as footsteps sounded down the hall. Her head jerked up, eyes wide.

"Someone's coming!"

Tom hastily shoved the files back into the compartment and closed it. He and Emily scanned the office, but there was nowhere to hide.

The footsteps grew louder, accompanied by voices. Tom's pulse pounded as he grabbed Emily's hand and pulled her down behind the desk. They huddled together, barely breathing, as the door opened.

Heavy footfalls entered along with two men's low voices. Tom recognized one as the mayor's.

"...keeping a close eye on things," the mayor was saying. "If there's evidence to be found, my team will find it first."

The other man chuckled. "And destroy it, I hope. We don't need anyone connecting this back to the development plans."

Tom and Emily exchanged shocked glances. The mayor was involved somehow.

"Oh, the evidence will disappear," the mayor assured him. "I just need a little more time to wrap this up neatly."

"See that you do," the other man said. "I can't have this murder interfering with my acquisition of that land. Your reelection campaign depends on it."

Tom's mind raced. The murder, the mayor, the land - it wasn't at all connected. He just needed this to disappear so he go on with another project.

He shifted slightly, straining to hear more. But Emily laid a warning hand on his arm. Discovery now could ruin everything. Clenching his fists, Tom forced himself to remain still.

After a few more vague threats, the men left. Tom and Emily huddled in the darkness, pulse pounding, waiting several minutes before finally creeping out.

"We need those files," Tom said grimly. "Let's get out of here before they come back."

Clutching the precious folders, they slipped away into the night. More determined than ever to crack this case wide open.

Emily's heels clicked sharply on the pavement as they hurried back to Tom's office, files in hand. The cool night air helped clear her head after the adrenaline rush of their close call at the mayor's office.

Beside her, Tom walked with purpose, jaw set. She could almost see the gears turning in his head as he processed all they had learned.

Once inside the worn wooden door bearing Tom's name, Emily let out a breath. Here, in this space that had become a second home, she felt safe.

Tom flipped on the desk lamp, washing the room in a warm glow. He carefully opened the file folder, revealing the life of Jonathan Reynolds in meticulous detail. Emily leaned in close, scanning the pages.

"JR Holdings," Tom mused, tapping the company name. "We thought the R was for Reynolds. But look..."

He slid out a document. Articles of incorporation for JR Holdings LLC. Signed by Jonathan Reynolds and...

"Ryan Simpson," Emily breathed. "Of course. Tom, the R is for Ryan!"

Tom nodded, a spark in his eyes. "Which means..."

"Jonathan wasn't in this alone," Emily finished. "He had a partner."

The threads of connection were coming together. Emily could feel they were on the cusp of a breakthrough.

Tom gazed at her, pride and affection mingling on his weathered face. "We're gonna get to the bottom of this, Em. I can feel it."

She smiled back softly. "Together, we will."

For a moment, all was still between them. Then Tom cleared his throat gruffly and turned back to the files. Emily blinked, trying to slow her suddenly racing heart.

They had a mystery to unravel first. The rest could wait.

Back home, Tom leaned back in his chair, rubbing his temples as he processed this new information. Having a partner complicated things, but it was a lead. A chance to finally get justice for Morgan and clear the LeBlanc siblings' names.

He glanced over at Emily, who was pacing slowly, brow furrowed in concentration. Her auburn hair shone in the lamplight, and Tom felt a familiar pang in his chest. After all these years, she still took his breath away. But this wasn't the time.

"Alright," he said. "We need to move fast. I say first thing tomorrow, we pay Mr. Ryan Simpson a little visit. Once we find him of course."

Emily nodded, a determined glint in her green eyes. "I agree. We'll catch him off guard, see if we can get him to slip up about his dealings with Reynolds."

She began gathering the files into a neat stack. Tom watched her graceful movements, wishing they could stay like this, working together late into the night. But the faster they solved this, the faster she'd be...

The sudden ring of his cell phone jarred him from his thoughts. Frowning, he glanced at the unknown number flashing across the screen.

"Tom Blackwell," he answered briskly.

"I have information about Morgan Reynolds' murder," said a garbled voice. "Meet me behind the old mill at sunset tomorrow. Come alone."

Before Tom could respond, the line went dead. He stared at the phone, pulse quickening. This could be dangerous, but it could also be the lead they needed.

"What is it?" Emily asked, concerned.

"Someone who claims to have information about Morgan's murder," Tom said. "Wants me to meet them at the old mill tomorrow at sunset."

Emily's eyes widened. "Tom...it has to be a trap."

"Maybe," he conceded. "Or maybe not. Either way, it's a risk I have to take."

Tom knew Emily wanted to argue, but he also knew she understood. For Morgan. For the children. They had to follow every lead. No matter where it took them.

Emily's brow furrowed as she considered Tom's words. This mysterious meeting could be a breakthrough, but it could also be extremely dangerous. As sheriff, her instinct was to protect Tom, but she also knew he was right - they had to pursue every lead, no matter the risk.

"Okay," she said finally, "but we do this together. I'm not letting you go alone."

Tom started to protest, but Emily silenced him with a look.

"No arguments. Wherever this goes, we go together." Her tone left no room for debate.

Tom nodded, a faint smile touching his lips. "Together then."

Emily felt a swell of emotion in her chest. In that moment, their fates were intertwined. Come what may, they would face it together.

She watched Tom gather his things, his strong hands deftly organizing the files on his desk. She knew those hands were equally capable of warmth and tenderness. Hands that made her feel safe.

As they walked to the door, Tom's hand found the small of her back, guiding her forward. The gesture anchored her to him, just as she hoped her presence gave him strength.

As Emily walked out she could see a young girl sitting atop the stairs in a nightgown. Clara was sitting in the stairs looking down on her with a smile.

CHAPTER 12

T he familiar musty scent of old books and leather furniture enveloped Tom as he stepped into his office. Shafts of late afternoon sun filtered through the blinds, casting bars of light across the crowded bookshelves and ornate mahogany desk. He paused, taking in the tense atmosphere.

Emily leaned against the desk, arms folded across her chest, auburn hair glowing in the sunlight. Her piercing green eyes met Tom's with an unspoken understanding. Cassidy sprawled across the leather couch, long legs dangling off the edge, thumbing through a heavy law book. Jack stood sentry by the window, brow furrowed in concentration as he reviewed his notes. The Leblanc siblings huddled together on the antique loveseat, their youthful faces etched with a mixture of fear and determination.

Tom cleared his throat, breaking the heavy silence. "Let's get started, shall we?" He moved towards his desk chair but remained standing, hands clasped behind his back in a familiar authoritative pose.

"Here's where we are so far. Jonathan says he was alone in his rental the night of the murder so his alibi is , more then weak."

He paused, letting the implication sink in. Cassidy looked up from her book, eyes wide. Emily nodded grimly.

"That mean Jonathan has opportunity. We also have multiple witnesses who saw an unknown car parked outside Morgan's house that night." Tom's voice was steady and precise, betraying none of the roiling emotion underneath.

Emily pushed off from the desk and began pacing, the click of her boots punctuating Tom's words. "If we can tie that car to him that would help but its still circumstantial evidence, we need more. Opportunity isn't enough - we need to establish means and motive."

Tom gazed at Emily, a flicker of admiration passing across his features. Twenty years had done nothing to diminish her fire. She was as determined as ever to find the truth, no matter what it cost...

Emily stopped pacing and turned to face the group, her piercing green eyes flashing with conviction.

"I don't believe for a second that Jonathan's relationship with Morgan was as rosy as he claims. He's always been possessive, controlling. Even back in high school." She paused, old memories surfacing. Shaking them off, she continued.

"I think if we dig deeper into his past, we'll find a pattern of manipulative behavior towards women. Morgan likely saw through his façade and tried to break things off. That would have made Jonathan desperate, angry...angry enough to kill. Plus we do have JR Holdings, the money owed to Morgan would be a great motive. If we could only find Ryan Simpson to tie it all together"

Emily's gaze swept over each person, as if daring them to contradict her. Cassidy looked thoughtful, while Tom gave an almost imperceptible nod.

"I can help with that." All eyes turned to Cassidy as she leaned forward eagerly, brushing a strand of chestnut hair behind her ear.

"I've been doing some digging online about Jonathan's background. Turns out he was engaged once before, to a woman named Rebecca. It ended badly when she accused him of stealing money from her family's business. He claimed innocence, but..." Cassidy trailed off meaningfully.

Emily crossed her arms. "That sounds like a pattern to me. We need to talk to this Rebecca, see what else she can tell us about his past. There's more to uncover here, I'm sure of it."

Cassidy and Tom murmured their agreement. The pieces were coming together, but they still had work to do. As the conversation continued, the team felt a renewed sense of purpose. Justice for Morgan was within their grasp.

The office fell silent as Emily and Cassidy finished speaking, the weight of their revelations sinking in. All eyes drifted to the corner where Clara and Charles sat, their youthful faces etched with somber maturity.

After a moment, Clara lifted her gaze, regarding each person before speaking in her characteristic eloquent tone.

"Jonathan was not as he seemed. His charm and charisma were merely masks, concealing his true nature. When Morgan allowed him into our lives, I was wary from the start."

She smoothed an imaginary wrinkle from her skirt, choosing her next words carefully. "He discouraged Morgan's family from visiting. He isolated her from friends, made her doubt herself. His control was subtle but persistent."

Charles nodded, his usual exuberance dimmed. "Yeah, he wanted it to be just the four of us. Like we were meant to be this perfect new family." His mouth twisted bitterly around the last word.

Clara placed a gentle hand on her brother's shoulder before continuing. "Over time, his grip on Morgan, and on us, tightened. We were helpless, until..."

Her voice faltered, eyes glistening. Emily leaned forward and squeezed her hand reassuringly.

"You've been so brave. We're going to make this right, I promise."

Clara took a shaky breath and managed a small smile at Emily's kindness. Their testimonies, though difficult, were bringing clarity.

Across the room, Jack listened pensively, his rugged features softened with empathy. As Clara's words faded, he cleared his throat gruffly.

"This is good work, getting all the pieces lined up. But we gotta be thorough, cover every angle. Are there others we should talk to, witnesses we've overlooked?"

He paused, brow furrowed in thought. "What about that fellow we found last week, the John Doe? He clearly knew something. But then he ended up dead in the harbor before we could meet. Fishy timing, no?"

Murmurs of assent rose around Jack's observation. They were making progress, yet there was still more evidence to pursue, more questions to answer, if they wanted to expose the truth. But they were determined, united in seeking justice for Morgan.

Tom leaned back in his office chair, steepling his fingers as he surveyed the determined faces around him. Despite the late hour, the air was charged with a renewed sense of purpose.

"You're right, Jack. We can't leave any stone unturned," Tom said finally, his gravelly voice slicing through the tension.

"It's time we go on the offensive. I say we put Jonathan under full surveillance - track his movements, monitor his communications. And we do full background checks, dig into his past relationships, business dealings, everything. There's more to uncover, I'm sure of it."

He slapped a hand on the desk for emphasis. "We build an airtight case, make it impossible for that snake to slither away from what he's done."

Emily nodded slowly, arms crossed as she considered Tom's words.

"Surveillance, background checks - that's a good start. But we need more eyes on this, more boots on the ground." She began pacing, brow furrowed.

"I'll reach out to some trusted officers, see who's willing to work with us on the down low, with the mayor huffing and puffing. The more coordination, the better our chances of taking Jonathan down."

She stopped and turned to Tom, green eyes blazing. "United we stand, divided we fall. We can't let that bastard drive a wedge between us. Together, we can make sure justice is served."

There were resolute murmurs around the room. They were wary of the challenges ahead, but ready to unite against the darkness looming over Oakwood. As long as they stood as one, the light of hope could not be extinguished.

Cassidy leaned forward in her chair, a determined glint in her eyes.

"I can help with the online research. Tracking down dirt on Jonathan and figuring out who else he might be connected to."

She cracked her knuckles dramatically. "Just get me on my computer and I'll work my magic. Creep's digital footprint won't know what hit it."

Tom nodded, a hint of pride mingling with concern on his craggy features. His daughter's skills never ceased to impress him, even as her involvement gave him pause.

"I appreciate that, Cass. But be smart - cover your tracks. Don't go poking hornets' nests until we know exactly what we're dealing with."

"Don't worry, Dad. I know how to fly under the radar." She gave him a reassuring smile. "I'll see what I can dig up on any shady connections from Jonathan's past. No one will even know I was there."

Satisfied with her response, Tom turned his attention to Nora. The elderly woman sat quietly, hands folded in her lap. She met his gaze with knowing eyes that had witnessed the passage of time and the secrets it revealed.

"Nora, I'd like you to tap into your network here in town. Use your discretion, but see what you can learn about any potential ties between Jonathan and others mixed up in Oakwood's criminal underbelly."

Nora nodded slowly, a determined edge to her gentle voice. "I'll shake the trees, see what falls out. My friends at the salon and bingo hall hear things, even if they don't realize the significance."

She patted Tom's hand reassuringly. "Leave it to me. I've got my ear to the ground better than anyone."

There were nods around the room. The battle lines were drawn, the assignments given. Together they would turn over every stone, follow every whisper, until the truth was uncovered.

Justice would not evade them.

Emily leaned forward in her chair, hands clasped on the table. Her emerald eyes were sharp with focus as she addressed the group.

"Jack and I need to bring the rest of the force up to speed on the investigation. We'll coordinate efforts to gather evidence and statements that can be used to build an airtight case."

Jack nodded in agreement. "With the whole department working together, we can cover more ground. I'll reach out to some old contacts at the state police too, see if they can lend a hand."

Emily gave him an approving look. "Good thinking. We need all hands on deck for this one." She turned her attention back to Tom. "In the meantime, keep us updated on anything you uncover. We'll do the same."

"You got it," Tom replied. "We'll compare notes and theories. Teamwork makes the dream work, right?"

That prompted a round of groans, cutting through the tension, with Cassidy pretending to vomit. Leave it to Tom and his corny dad jokes. For a moment, the strain lifted, smiles emerging at the welcome bit of levity.

Sobering, Tom swept his gaze over the collected faces. "Let's get to it then. We all have our jobs to do." He stood, the others rising with him. "It's time to bring Morgan's killer to justice. For her...and for her kids."

There were solemn nods, spines straightening with renewed purpose. The briefing concluded, they began to disperse, resolve etched into their features. The day was fading, but their work had just begun. Darkness would not deter them from their quest for the truth.

Tom watched his makeshift team head out, pride swelling in his chest. They were a motley crew, but bonded by a shared goal—to protect this town and its people.

Emily paused at the door, meeting his eyes with a knowing look. No words were needed. Come hell or high water, they'd see this through together. With a final nod, she headed out into the deepening dusk.

Beside Tom, Cassidy gathered up her laptop, notes scattered haphazardly across his desk. "I'll dig into Jonathan's background tonight, Dad. There's got to be something online we can use."

"I know you'll find it if there is." He squeezed her shoulder. "But don't stay up too late, okay? You need your rest."

She rolled her eyes good-naturedly. "Yes, Dad."

As she left, the Leblanc siblings trailed after her, Clara's hand clasped in Charles' protective grip. Tom's heart ached, remembering their stricken faces at the crime scene. They'd endured so much, but with Morgan gone, the future was uncertain.

He crouched down. "You two take care of each other, all right? We're going to make this right."

Charles nodded, eyes overbright. Clara managed a trembling smile. Tom ruffled their hair and sent them on their way, wishing he could shelter them from all this. But the best he could do was find the truth and a huge hug.

Alone now, Tom gazed out the window overlooking Main Street. Dusk settled over Oakwood like a blanket, streetlights winking on one by one. Somewhere out there, a killer lurked in the shadows. But no darkness could withstand the light for long. And Tom aimed to shine a blinding beam on the culprit, exposing their misdeeds for all to see.

The hunt was on. Justice would be served. Tom would make damn sure of it.

CHAPTER 14

Tom stepped into the darkness of the old Mill, the blood roaring in his ears. Shadows danced across the walls as his flashlight cut through the gloom. Something skittered away into the corners. He swept the beam slowly to the left, then right. Clear. For now.

He spoke barely above a whisper. "I'm going in."

Outside, Emily nodded, her knuckles white on the grip of her Glock. Beside her, Jack shifted, his knees cracking. Waiting. Listening.

Tom crept deeper into the belly of the Mill, senses straining. Here and there, shapes emerged from the dark as the flashlight found them - abandoned crates, rusted chains, cobwebs stringing across rafters like ghostly lace.

Each step took effort to control, quiet. He paused, breathing deep to still the trembling in his chest. He pictured his grandpa at the helm of their little boat, hand on Tom's shoulder, the briny scent of the sea in the air. "Steady on, boy," he'd said. Tom moved forward once more, steadied.

Suddenly, a loud crack split the air. Tom whirled, gun raised. Had they found him already? A tense moment passed. Then a pigeon burst from the rafters, disappearing through a broken window. Tom's heartbeat slowed. Still clear. But anything could lurk within this hungry darkness. He had to be ready.

Outside, Emily peered into the gloom, willing Tom to appear. She thought of his strong arms wrapped around her, the warmth of his breath on her neck. Come back to me, she pleaded silently. Jack shifted again, eyes scanning the perimeter. Ever watchful. Ever patient.

The three of them suspended in stillness, bound by loyalty and love, while the secrets of the Mill waited to be discovered in the darkness.

Tom swept the flashlight beam slowly across the floor, searching for any clues among the debris. His eyes narrowed as the light glinted off something small and metallic nestled in the dusty shadows. He crouched down and carefully picked it up, turning it over in his hand. A cufflink - tarnished silver etched with the initials R.S.

Tom's pulse quickened as he realized this could be a vital piece of evidence, connecting the mill to his prime suspect. He quickly slipped the cufflink into a small evidence bag and secured it in his pocket, knowing he had to get this to forensics as soon as possible.

As he rose, Emily's voice suddenly crackled through his earpiece. "Tom, what's your status? Did you find anything?" Though muted by static, her tone was laced with concern.

Tom lifted the mic to his lips and whispered, "I've got something. A cufflink, initials R.S. Could be a solid lead."

"Good work, but proceed with extreme caution," Emily urged. "We don't know what other surprises might be waiting in there."

Tom's jaw tightened with determination. "Copy that. I'll keep you posted."

Slipping the mic back into his pocket, Tom swept the flashlight around once more. The dancing shadows seemed to taunt him, concealing dangers unknown. But he had come too far to turn back now. Steeling himself, Tom ventured deeper into the mill's ominous darkness.

Tom moved cautiously through the cavernous old mill, his footsteps echoing eerily in the vast empty space. Shadows danced across the cracked concrete walls as his flashlight beam bobbed ahead of him. He swept it slowly from side to side, searching for any sign of movement or clues left behind.

The air was heavy with the scent of damp and mold, hints of rust and oil lingering from the mill's heyday. Tom's senses strained, catching every creak and groan of the building settling around him. He paused, shining his light down a narrow passageway leading to a rusted metal staircase. Where did it lead? His curiosity was piqued, but Emily's warning echoed in his mind. Proceed with caution.

Edging toward the passage, Tom tested each step as if walking through a minefield. The staircase groaned under his weight, protesting the intrusion. He swept his light upward, trailing along the stairs to a small loft area tucked under the rafters. If there were answers to be found, they could very well be hidden up there.

Tom took another step forward when suddenly a loud crash reverberated through the mill. He froze, snapping off his flashlight and pressing himself against the cold concrete wall. His heart hammered as the sound faded, leaving only deafening silence in its wake.

Tom held his breath, every muscle tense as he strained to detect any further sounds. Had it just been the old building settling or shifting? Or was there someone else lurking in the shadows?

He waited a beat longer, then clicked his flashlight back on. The beam cut through the darkness as he slowly peeled himself off the wall and continued toward the metal staircase. Each step upward produced a haunting creak, but Tom kept climbing until he reached the small loft area.

Cobwebs draped across the corners and beams, undisturbed for ages. His light swept over a few old crates and an antique desk tucked against the far wall. Tom moved cautiously toward it, noticing the scattering of papers across its surface. His eyes narrowed as he focused on a faded photograph lying amidst the mess. Two familiar faces stared back at him, though much younger.

"Tom?" Emily's voice suddenly crackled through his earpiece, making him flinch. "You okay in there? Anything?"

Tom let out a slow breath, steadying his nerves. "I'm alright. Found something interesting up here actually. I'll tell you more once I'm out."

"Copy that," Emily replied. "We've got your six, just say the word."

Tom nodded, even knowing she couldn't see him. Her reassurance grounded him, bringing his racing mind back into focus. Answers first, then they could plan their next move. With renewed purpose, Tom began photographing the documents, trusting that the secrets they held would soon be revealed.

The beam from Tom's flashlight cut through the gloom as he stepped farther into the hidden room. Dust danced in the air, swirling in the wake of his movement. His eyes were immediately drawn to the antique desk tucked against the far wall. Stacks of faded papers and mildewed books covered its surface, hinting at the secrets that lay hidden within their crumbling pages.

As Tom approached, his pulse quickened. This remote space within the old mill could hold the key to unraveling the truth behind the Oakwood Tragedy. With great care, he sifted through the documents, searching for any mention of Jonathan Reynolds or Ryan Simpson. The years had rendered some of the ink barely legible, but Tom squinted to make out names and dates that might prove critical.

Outside, Emily paced restlessly, casting frequent glances toward the door. Her brows were furrowed with concern, internally debating whether to check on Tom. Jack placed a steadying hand on her shoulder.

"He'll be alright, Em. Tom's got this." His tone was reassuring, yet his tight expression betrayed his own worries.

Emily sighed. "I know. I just wish we could see what's happening in there. What if he needs backup?"

Jack gave her shoulder a squeeze. "Then we'll be ready. But for now, we wait."

Emily nodded, resisting the urge to reach for her radio. She had to trust Tom, but dread still twisted in her gut. All she could do was hope the documents held the break they desperately needed before darkness fell once more over Oakwood.

Tom's breath caught in his throat as his gaze fell upon a faded photograph tucked between the crumbling pages. Two familiar faces smiled up at him, seemingly without a care in the world. But Tom knew better.

Jonathan Reynolds had his arm slung casually around a younger Ryan Simpson, their grinning expressions masking a sinister bond. Tom's pulse pounded as the implication sunk in - Ryan's involvement ran deeper than they realized.

With slightly unsteady hands, Tom quickly snapped photos of the damning evidence. Proof of the connection he long suspected but could never confirm, now tangible before his eyes. He had to show Emily and Jack immediately.

Tucking the photograph safely into his pocket, Tom hurried from the room, mind racing. How long had Ryan been tied to Reynolds' criminal network? What other secrets lurked in his past? Tom's shock quickly hardened into resolve. The time for truth had come.

He emerged into moonlight and headed straight for Emily and Jack. Their faces mirrored his own grave expression.

"I found something." Tom's voice was tight. "A photo, linking Ryan to Reynolds years back. We need to move, now. Before word gets back to Ryan about us being here."

Emily and Jack exchanged urgent looks. Then Emily spoke, authority ringing in her tone.

"Let's go. We'll regroup at the station and plan our next steps." She placed a hand briefly on Tom's shoulder. "Good work in there."

Tom nodded, adrenaline coursing through his veins. The hunt for answers had only just begun. But with his team at his side, he was ready to face whatever darkness emerged as they pulled at the threads of Oakwood's past. The truth would not evade them for long.

Emily led the way to the patrol cars, gravel crunching under their hurried footsteps. As they climbed in and pulled onto the coast road, Tom's mind continued racing.

"We need to get a warrant and search Ryan's home and office," he said. "There could be more evidence there linking him to Reynolds."

Jack nodded from the driver's seat. "I'll call Judge Kendall as soon as we get back. Shouldn't be a problem getting a warrant with that photo."

"Good. And we should-" Tom's words cut off as the crackle of the radio pierced the air.

"Sheriff Foster, we have more info on the John Doe we found as requested."

Tom and Jack exchanged startled looks. Emily grabbed the radio.

"Yes Dispatch, Sheriff Foster here what do we have?"

CHAPTER 15

The office was bathed in the golden glow of the setting sun as Tom gazed out the window, the weight of disappointment heavy on his shoulders. Around him, the team sank into chairs, the usual banter replaced by somber silence.

Emily perched on the edge of Tom's desk, arms folded across her chest. "I know this feels like a setback, but it's not over yet. We'll find another way to get Jonathan."

Tom turned from the window, jaw clenched. "Finding John Doe's real identity was our best shot. Without that evidence..." He trailed off, raking a hand through his hair.

"So we go to plan B. Or C. Or Z. We don't stop until we get justice for Morgan and the kids." Emily's voice was steady, but Tom could see the flicker of doubt in her eyes. This case had already taken so much out of her. Out of all of them.

Tom moved to his chair and eased down into it with a tired sigh, the old leather creaking familiarly. This office held so many memories, good and bad. He thought of all the cases he and Emily had tackled together over the years, in this very room.

They'd had setbacks before, but they'd always found a way through together.

He looked up at Emily's determined face, remembering the idealistic rookie she'd been when they'd first met. They'd both aged, the job having taken its toll, but that relentless sense of duty was still there.

Tom allowed himself a small smile. "You're right. We dust ourselves off and keep going. For the kids' sake."

Emily nodded, resolve hardening her features. "We owe them that much."

Tom glanced around at the team, seeing his own conviction reflected back. They would keep fighting, for as long as it took. The truth was out there, and they would find it.

Tom leaned forward in his chair, steepling his fingers as his brow furrowed in concentration.

"Alright team, this is a setback but it's not the end. We need to go back over everything we know and look for a new angle."

He began ticking off points on his fingers.

"One - the DNA results confirm the John Doe is Ryan Simpson. That closes off one avenue of investigation, but it doesn't negate the other evidence we've uncovered. We still know he worked Jonathan, the car, the unkown prints maybe they're his?"

Tom paused, tapping his chin thoughtfully.

"Two - we still have the foster kids' statements placing Jonathan at the scene. That gives us an eyewitness account, even if we can't corroborate it yet."

He stood up and began pacing, his movements sharp and purposeful.

"Three - we need to connect the murder weapon to Jonathan. then we will have means and opportunity, we have the motive."

Tom stopped and turned to Emily, his eyes blazing.

"There's still a path forward here. We dig deeper into Jonathan's past, shake the trees until something falls out. I want phone records, financials, background on his relationships - everything."

Emily nodded slowly, but Tom could see the hesitation in her eyes. She worried they were grasping at straws, putting the kids at risk on a hunch. This case had already taken so much out of her.

But they owed it to Morgan, and to Charles and Clara, to see this through. Tom knew Emily would keep fighting, even if it put her own safety on the line. Her relentless sense of duty wouldn't allow her to back down.

Not until they got justice.

* * *

Josh sat at the counter of Nora's Diner, absently stirring his coffee as he stared down at the letter in his hand. The Harvard seal stared back at him, seeming to mock his dreams.

"We regret to inform you..." the first line read.

He had thought his essay was strong, that it really captured his passion for literature and desire to study it further. But it wasn't enough.

Josh sighed, the sting of rejection hitting him anew. Getting into Harvard had been his goal for years, ever since he discovered his love of reading and writing. Now it felt like that door had slammed shut on him.

The jingle of the entrance bell pulled Josh from his thoughts. He looked up to see Cassidy bounding over, her wavy hair bouncing with each step.

"Hey you," she said, sliding into the booth across from him. Her smile faded when she saw the defeated look on Josh's face.

"I'm guessing it wasn't good news?" she asked gently.

Josh slid the letter over in response. Cassidy scanned it quickly, then reached out to squeeze his hand.

"I'm really sorry, Josh. I'm really really sorry, we'll find another way I'm sure."

He nodded, not trusting his voice to remain steady. Cassidy seemed to sense he needed a moment, so she just sat with him in silence.

After a few minutes, Josh cleared his throat. "I really thought I had a shot, you know? But I guess it wasn't meant to be."

Cassidy tilted her head, regarding him thoughtfully. "Maybe this wasn't your path right now. But that doesn't mean you should give up. You have so much talent - I know you'll find success with it one day."

Despite his sadness, Josh felt a glimmer of hope at her encouragement. No matter what life threw at him, he could always count on Cassidy to lift him up. But this also meant Cassidy would be gone and he wouldn't be coming.

✽ ✽ ✽

The next morning, Tom stood gazing out the window of his office, watching the boats bob gently in the harbor as he gathered his thoughts. The revelations about Ryan's true identity had thrown their investigation into turmoil, but he refused to let Jonathan slip through their grasp.

A knock at the door shook him from his contemplation. Emily entered, her auburn hair swept back in a ponytail that accentuated the determination in her green eyes.

"Morning," Tom said gruffly. "The others here yet?"

"Just pulled in," Emily replied. She crossed her arms, mirroring Tom's pensive body language. "So where do we go from here?"

Before Tom could respond, the door opened again and Josh, Cassidy, and Nora filed in. Tom motioned for them to grab seats around the conference table.

"I know we're all reeling from the news about Ryan," Tom began. "But we can't let this setback stop us from getting justice for the Leblanc kids."

Nora nodded firmly. "Those poor children have been through enough. We need to keep digging."

"But with our main lead gone, where do we even start?" Josh asked.

Cassidy placed a hand on his arm. "We'll figure it out. One step at a time."

Emily began pacing, a familiar signal of her razor-sharp mind kicking into gear. "Maybe we've been looking at this wrong. We've focused so much on Ryan that we haven't fully investigated other angles."

She turned to Tom, her eyes alight. "It's time we took a closer look at Morgan's inner circle. There were others who might have wanted her gone."

Tom felt a spark of hope reignite within him. Emily was right - they needed to widen the scope of their investigation.

"Good thinking," he said. "We'll start interviewing Morgan's close friends and colleagues. Someone knows something they're not telling us."

The team exchanged determined glances. The path forward remained unclear, but their resolve to uncover the truth and deliver justice was as strong as ever. With renewed motivation, they dove back into the case files, searching for the clue that would break this investigation wide open.

❊ ❊ ❊

Josh sat alone in his bedroom, struggling to process the day's revelations. He glanced at the rejection letter from Harvard, the official stamp seeming to mock his dreams. First the scholarship, now this. He felt like everything was slowly slipping away.

Josh opened his journal, seeking solace in the one thing that still made sense - his writing. He began pouring his emotions onto the blank pages, finding catharsis in giving voice to his pain and frustration.

He wrote about his anger at the injustice of it all. The Leblanc siblings didn't deserve this living nightmare. His mom didn't deserve to be killed for doing what she thought was right. And Morgan Reynolds certainly didn't deserve her life to be cut short so violently.

As the words flowed, Josh started to feel a sense of calm wash over him. He knew that no matter how bleak things seemed, he couldn't give up. The truth was out there somewhere and he would keep searching for it, using his voice to speak for those who no longer could.

* * *

Emily leaned against the railing of the pier, gazing out at the moonlit ocean as it lapped gently against the shore. The soft breeze carried the scent of brine and stirred her auburn hair, providing a moment of stillness she so desperately needed.

It had been a tumultuous few weeks since they reopened the investigation into Morgan's murder. While exhuming the truth was noble in purpose, Emily couldn't ignore the toll it had taken. Lives had been disrupted, relationships tested, reputations questioned - and for what? Just when they seemed on the cusp of a breakthrough, the rug was pulled out from under them.

Emily wondered if she had led them all astray. Were the risks worth the cost of pursuing justice? She thought of Tom and the pain this caused him having to defend his friend against the weight of circumstantial evidence. Of Cassidy and Josh, whose family was fracturing before their eyes. And the Leblanc siblings, whose hope for freedom could be slipping away.

Lost in thought, Emily didn't hear Tom's approaching footsteps. He joined her at the railing, the breeze ruffling his salt-and-pepper hair. For a moment, neither spoke, both finding solace in the rhythmic splash of waves.

Finally, Tom broke the silence. "I know a feeling of defeat when I see one. But this isn't over yet."

Emily turned to face him. The steely glint of determination in Tom's grey-blue eyes reignited her own resolve. If he could cling to hope, so could she.

"You're right," Emily said. "We can't give up when we've come this far. What's our next move?"

CHAPTER 16

Tom stared blankly at the stacks of papers and case files strewn across his cluttered desk, rubbing his temples as doubt and uncertainty weighed heavily on his mind. Josh sat on the corner couch in the room, both men seeming defeated and basking in each others gloom. The details of the Oakwood Tragedy swirled in Tom thoughts, tangled and complex, and he wondered if justice could ever truly be served for the innocent lives shattered in its wake. Josh contemplating his recent academic rejection.

The creak of the office door stirred Tom from his spiraling thoughts. He glanced up to see Emily entering, her auburn hair glowing in the lamp light, green eyes dark with concern. She crossed the room and placed a gentle but firm hand on Tom's shoulder.

"This case has rattled us all," Emily said, her voice soft but steady. "But I know that tenacious flame still burns inside you, Tom. The one that won't rest until the truth is uncovered."

Tom sighed, the lines on his weathered face deepening. "I want to believe that, Em. But there are so many unanswered questions. So many lives hanging in the balance."

"Hey." Emily's grip tightened, her eyes boring intensely into his. "You've taken on far greater challenges than this and found justice. Have faith in the gifts God gave you. Your intellect. Your integrity. Your heart."

Tom nodded slowly, the fog of uncertainty beginning to lift from his mind. Emily's words washed over him like the first rays of dawn, kindling his determination. She was right - he'd sworn an oath to protect this town, no matter the cost.

With renewed conviction, Tom rose from his desk. The weight of doubt still tugged at him, but standing beside Emily, he now had the strength to push forward. To unravel the dark threads of this tragedy until the truth was revealed. Until justice could finally be served.

The door to Tom's office burst open again, and Cassidy Blackwell bounded in with her characteristic exuberance.

"Sorry to interrupt," she said, though her grin indicated she was anything but. Cassidy's vibrant energy instantly dispelled the somber mood that had permeated the room just moments before.

She turned to Josh. "I've been thinking - you should try to get a football scholarship to Harvard! I know you've got your heart set on English lit, but your skills on the field could be your ticket in. Show those Ivy League snobs you're more than just a meathead jock."

Josh hesitated, his brow furrowing. "I dunno, Cass. Football was never my true passion - just something to kill time until college. And I'd hate to get stuck with that label, you know?"

He sighed, running a hand through his tousled blond hair. "Maybe I'm better off leaving that part behind. Trying to get in on my own merits instead of chasing some sports scholarship."

Cassidy frowned, undeterred. She stepped closer, her blue eyes brimming with sincerity.

"Don't sell yourself short, Josh. You've got so much untapped potential - on the field and off. This could open up so many doors for you."

She placed a hand on his shoulder. "Trust me. Your talent and heart are what matter most. You've got so much to offer Harvard, in ways they can't even imagine yet."

Josh managed a small smile, bolstered by her encouragement. "Thanks, Cass. You always know just what to say."

From his desk, Tom observed their interaction, pride swelling in his chest. His daughter had become a fine young woman - one capable of inspiring others. And though the future remained uncertain, Tom now had faith that together, they would find their way through the darkness.

Josh took a deep breath, considering Cassidy's words. She had a point - football could be his stepping stone, a means to an end. With his skills, he likely could earn a scholarship to an Ivy

League school. But did he really want to commit to 4 more years of practices, drills, conditioning? His true passion had always been literature. Ever since he was young, Josh had found solace between the pages of a good book. The words transported him to fantastical worlds where anything was possible.

"You really think I could leverage football to study English at Harvard?" he asked hesitantly.

Cassidy's eyes lit up. "Absolutely! You'd bring such a unique perspective to both fields. Your talent on the field and your passion for books - that's what will make you stand out."

She gave his arm an encouraging squeeze. "This is your chance to chase your dreams, Josh. Take a risk and see where it leads."

From across the room, Tom observed his daughter's sincere attempts to inspire Josh. Though outwardly stoic, a hint of a smile tugged at his lips. He always marveled at Cassidy's ability to connect with others on such a deep level. She had a gift for seeing potential in people that they often couldn't see themselves. It reminded Tom so much of his late wife, Cassidy's mother. She too had possessed that same spirit - a contagious zest for life that uplifted those around her.

Seeing Cassidy encourage Josh, Tom swelled with pride. His daughter was well on her way to becoming a strong, compassionate woman. And no matter what challenges lay ahead, Tom knew they would face them together, united by an unbreakable bond.

Emily watched the exchange between Cassidy and Josh, her green eyes radiating warmth. She could see the profound connection between the two - a depth of caring that brought out their best qualities.

Josh took a deep breath, shifting his gaze between Cassidy and Tom. Cassidy's words had struck a chord, awakening possibilities he'd been afraid to consider. A football scholarship to Harvard...it could open so many doors while still allowing him to nurture his literary passions. The more Josh pondered the idea, the more his doubts gave way to growing excitement.

He met Cassidy's earnest blue eyes again. In them he saw belief - belief in him and his potential. With newfound resolve, Josh gave a nod.

"Let's do it," he said. "I'll apply for that football scholarship to Harvard."

Cassidy's face lit up. She pulled Josh into an enthusiastic hug.

"You've got this!" she exclaimed.

Over Cassidy's shoulder, Josh caught Emily's approving gaze. Her expression reflected the pride and hope swelling in his own heart.

With his girlfriend's encouragement and Emily's steadfast support, Josh felt empowered to pursue his dreams to their fullest potential. The future seemed brighter than ever before.

Tom slowly rose from his desk, a renewed sense of purpose shining in his piercing blue-grey eyes. After weeks of frustration and doubt, he finally felt the fog lifting. Emily's unwavering support and Cassidy's insight had been just what he needed to regain motivation.

"Thank you, Emily," he said, meeting her striking green gaze. "I don't know what I'd do without you."

Turning to Cassidy, he squeezed her shoulder affectionately. "And thank you for the energy, kiddo. You really gave me a fresh perspective."

Cassidy grinned, always happy to help her dad any way she could.

Together, the four of them moved to stand in a close circle, hands clasped. Tom looked from Emily's strength, to Cassidy's spirit, to the new hope in Josh's eyes. In that moment, all his doubts washed away. With his family beside him, he could take on any challenge.

"I won't let you down," Tom promised them. "We're going to see this through...together."

Their hands tightened, a pulse of unity passing between them. No matter what lay ahead, they would face it as one - bound by devotion, trust, and love.

Emily's eyes softened as she gazed at Tom, a hint of mistiness in them. Though she hid it well behind her tough exterior, seeing the man she loved regain his spirit brought her profound relief and joy.

After all these years, through the ups and downs, their bond had only grown stronger. Tom was her rock, her shelter in the storm. With him by her side, she could weather anything.

A silent look passed between them, speaking volumes that words could not capture. It acknowledged the depth of their connection - one forged in fire, tested by time, and unbreakable. Come what may, they would stand united.

Hands still clasped, they turned towards the door. Cassidy and Josh fell in step beside them, the four walking out together into the golden light of late afternoon.

Though uncertainty still loomed on the horizon, they now felt ready to meet it head-on. Each step was filled with renewed purpose and determination, their strides steady and sure.

As they stepped outside, a cool breeze rustled the turning leaves and tousled their hair. Gazing at the beauty around them, they drew strength from this place they called home. Its timeless rhythms anchored them.

With one last exchanged glance, they fanned out down the sidewalk and went their separate ways, ready to play their parts in untangling the dark mysteries that lay beneath Oakwood's tranquil surface.

Though apart, their unbreakable bonds remained, tying them together even when out of sight. No matter what revelations awaited, or how the danger escalated, they would have each other's backs.

CHAPTER 17

The dim light of the backroom cast ominous shadows across Tom's clenched fists. Beside him, Emily's eyes narrowed with steely determination as Jonathan emerged from the darkness.

"We know what you did," Tom said, his voice unwavering.

Jonathan halted, the confident smile freezing on his face. Tom saw a flicker of unease in the man's eyes. Good. Let him squirm.

"I'm not sure what you mean," Jonathan said smoothly. Too smoothly. "If this is about Morgan—"

"Cut the act," Tom snapped. His hands flexed, knuckles whitening. "We found your purchase of gas with the dark car, the receipt from Oakwood Gas, with Ryan Simpson's car. Your alibi doesn't check out."

Jonathan's facade cracked, lips parting in surprise. Got him. Tom pressed his advantage, laying out each damning piece of evidence. Jonathan scrambled, words flowing like oil as he tried to explain it all away. But Tom could see the desperation in the man's eyes.

Emily stepped forward, green eyes piercing. "We found Morgan's bracelet."

The color drained from Jonathan's face. His hands twitched at his sides, the urge to run written in every taut muscle. But there was nowhere to go. Nowhere to hide from the truth.

Tom's heart swelled as he watched the man who had shattered their community struggle beneath the weight of his lies. They still had a long road ahead. But finally, Morgan could rest in peace. And maybe, just maybe, their little Oakwood could feel whole again.

Jonathan's composure cracked as Emily revealed the damning evidence. His confident facade melted away, leaving behind a man scrambling for escape.

"That...that doesn't prove anything," he stammered, though the lie was evident in his darting eyes and trembling hands.

Emily stepped closer, unwavering. "It proves you were in her car. Right before she died."

Jonathan shrank back. "I-I can explain—"

"Save it," Tom cut in, fists clenched. The time for lies was over. "We know you killed her. Just tell us why."

Silence hung heavy. Jonathan's lips moved wordlessly as he grasped for plausible deniability. But nothing could erase the truth—he was cornered.

Revulsion rose in Tom's gut. To take a life over something so petty...it turned his stomach. Morgan had been family. And this monster had stolen her away.

Emily's voice remained steady, though Tom could see the fire in her eyes. "So you decided to play judge and executioner. You robbed those kids of the only real home they'd known."

Jonathan flinched at the accusation. Good—let the weight of his sins torment him.

"Was it worth it?" Tom asked bitterly. "Was it worth killing?"

Jonathan said nothing, but his face told the story. He may have fooled others with his charm and wit, but the mask was off. Here stood a small, pitiful man who valued his pride over human life.

Tom took a step closer, his fists clenched at his sides. "It's over, Jonathan. No more lies. No more games." His voice was hard as steel. "You're going to confess everything - right here, right now."

Jonathan shrank back, eyes darting around the room. He looked like a cornered animal. "Now wait just a minute," he sputtered. "Let's not get ahead of ourselves..."

But Emily cut him off. "Don't even try it," she snapped. "We know you were there that night. We have the evidence to prove it." Her unwavering gaze bore into him. "So start talking."

Finally, he slumped in resignation, all pretenses gone. When he spoke, his voice was flat and empty. "I never meant to hurt her. But she was pushing for money, I needed money. I couldn't let that happen."

Tom's jaw clenched. An apology could never make things right. "Keep going," he said sharply.

Jonathan's breath quickened. "That night...I just wanted to talk to her. To make her see reason." His eyes took on a faraway look. "But when she opened the door, I just...lost control." His voice dropped to a horrified whisper. "There was so much blood..."

Revulsion churned inside Tom. This monster had robbed Morgan's life in a fit of rage. And the children - Charles and Clara - their lives forever scarred.

Emily's voice rang out firmly. "Her blood is on your hands, Jonathan. Now it's time you paid for what you've done."

Jonathan lifted his head, resignation in his eyes. The weight of his sins had finally caught up with him. And justice would soon be served.

Jonathan's eyes darted around the room, searching for an escape as the realization sank in that there was no talking his way out of this. Tom and Emily stood resolutely between him and the door, their stances showing they were prepared for any sudden movements.

Jonathan scrambled backwards, knocking over a chair. "No...no! I won't go to prison for this!"

In a blur of motion, he snatched a letter opener off the desk and lunged at Emily. She sidestepped smoothly, using his momentum against him to send him stumbling past her. Tom was on him in an instant, wrenching the makeshift weapon from his grasp and forcing him down onto the floor.

Jonathan thrashed against Tom's hold, cursing and spitting. "Let me go, damn you!"

Tom kept him pinned, jaw clenched. "Not a chance."

Emily grabbed Jonathan's arms, swiftly cuffing his wrists behind his back. Her green eyes blazed with anger. "Attacking an officer? You just can't stop making things worse for yourself."

Jonathan let out a strangled cry, finally going limp in defeat. The fight had gone out of him.

Tom released his grip and stood, lip curled in disgust. "I hope you rot for what you've done."

Emily nodded, hauling Jonathan to his feet. "You're going to pay for every life you've ruined."

As they led him firmly from the room, Jonathan could only stare blankly ahead, the weight of his sins leaving him hollow inside. Justice had caught up at last.

Jonathan slumped into the chair, all bravado draining from his face. He dropped his head into his hands, finally broken.

Emily shook her head in disgust. "You took her life over your own cowardice."

Jonathan had no response. The truth, at last laid bare, was condemnation enough.

Emily stepped forward, resolve in her eyes. "Your confession gives Morgan's memory justice. Now it's time you faced the consequences."

Tom nodded. The winding path had led to the truth. Morgan could finally rest in peace.

Tom's piercing eyes remained fixed on Jonathan as he firmly clasped the man's arm, ensuring he could not slip away before the authorities arrived. Though they had secured a confession, Tom knew better than to let his guard down - Jonathan had proven himself a master of deception and manipulation.

Beside him, Emily straightened her posture, the glint of her sheriff's badge catching the dim light. Her face was stoic, but Tom could detect the hint of satisfied relief in her gaze. After weeks tracking half-truths and dead ends, justice was finally within reach.

"I'm calling this in," Emily said briskly, pulling out her phone. "The evidence we've collected, paired with his full confession, will ensure maximum charges."

Tom nodded. "I'll keep watch here. Once backup arrives we can transfer him to the county jail." His tone made it clear Jonathan would not be getting away.

Emily began dialing, keeping her eyes fixed on their captive. "Oakwood PD, this is Sheriff Foster. We need immediate assistance at..."

As she relayed the details, Tom tightened his grip on Jonathan's arm. The man remained eerily silent, the fight seeming to have left him. Tom knew better than to believe his resigned facade - he would be ready to bolt at the first chance.

But neither he nor Emily would let that happen. They would see this through. Justice would be served for Morgan, and for the town that had suffered this heinous crime. The winding path had led them here, and they would not falter.

Tom released a heavy sigh as Emily ended the call, the weight of the night's events settling over him. Though they had succeeded in getting justice for Morgan, the toll of the investigation was undeniable. Emily turned to him, her shoulders slumping slightly as the adrenaline began to ebb.

"It's finally over," Tom said quietly. "Or at least, this part is."

Emily nodded, her voice softening. "We did it. We got him. Morgan can rest easy now."

She paused, meeting Tom's tired but satisfied gaze. In that shared look was an unspoken acknowledgement of all they had endured to reach this point. The leads that went nowhere, the sleepless nights parsing evidence, the slowly unraveling web of lies until the truth was laid bare. It had tested them, but they had risen to the challenge.

Tom scrubbed a hand over his face, feeling the rasp of stubble. "I'm ready to get out of here. Grab a stiff drink at McGinty's, try to..." He trailed off, emotion constricting his throat.

"I know," Emily said gently. "But we've got a job to finish first."

She glanced over at Jonathan. The man sat slumped against the wall, defeated. Tom followed her gaze and straightened, re-focusing on the task at hand.

Soon the approaching wail of sirens pierced the night. Back-up had arrived. With a deep breath, Tom steeled himself to see this through. There would be statements to give, evidence to hand over, justice to be enacted.

For now, they had done their part. The rest could come later.

Side by side, he and Emily made their way to the door. As they stepped out into the cool night air, Tom felt the burden on his shoulders lift ever so slightly. It was not gone fully, not yet - but for the first time in weeks, he could breathe again.

Tom paused on the front steps, taking in a deep breath of the crisp night air. It was laden with the briny scent of the nearby ocean and the loamy fragrance of fallen leaves. Autumn had arrived in Oakwood, and with it, a new season was dawning for them all.

He glanced over at Emily, her auburn hair shining in the moonlight. Though her face was drawn, her green eyes reflected a glimmer of hope. They still had a long road ahead, but the revelations of tonight marked a turning point.

Tom took her hand, giving it a gentle, reassuring squeeze. No matter what came next, they would face it together. Cassidy too, though the events of the past weeks had shaken her world, was resilient. She would recover, her spirit perhaps stronger for having weathered the storm.

In the distance, the beams of flashlights danced between the trees as more officers approached. Soon they would have to recount the details, relive each moment again. But that could wait.

For now, Tom let the quiet sounds of Oakwood wash over him— the whisper of wind through the pines, the lapping of waves on shore. This was still home, still the place he loved. They would rebuild, restore what had been damaged, make it whole again.

The truth was out, shadows exposed to light. A long process of healing could finally begin. As Tom stood gazing at the stars, he felt the first small stirrings of hope for the future.

CHAPTER 18

T he town square buzzed with excitement as Sheriff Emily Foster led a handcuffed Jonathan up the steps of the courthouse. A crowd had gathered, eager to witness the long-awaited arrest of Morgan's real killer. Emily maintained her stoic expression, though inside, relief washed over her like the ocean tide. Justice would finally be served.

As Jonathan disappeared inside, the onlookers erupted into cheers and applause. Tears of joy streamed down the faces of many who had known Morgan. Others hugged their loved ones, the dark cloud that had been cast over Oakwood finally lifting.

Emily scanned the crowd, spotting Tom standing off to the side, pride gleaming in his eyes. She made her way over to him, the hint of a smile tugging at her lips.

"We did it," she said.

Tom nodded, overcome with emotion. "It's finally over."

He opened his arms and Emily stepped into his embrace. She pressed her cheek against his chest, listening to the steady beat of his heart as he held her close.

In that moment, the rest of the world faded away. The months of lies, betrayal and anguish melted into the past. All that remained was the two of them, together again. Tom gently stroked her hair and she clung tighter, never wanting to let go.

"I'm so proud of you," he murmured into her ear. Emily's eyes watered at his words. No matter how difficult things had been between them, Tom had never lost faith in her. With him by her side, she felt like she could take on anything.

Emily lifted her head to meet his tender gaze, her fingers trailing down his rugged jawline.

"I wouldn't have made it through this without you," she said, her voice thick with emotion.

Tom gave her that crooked smile she adored. "Sure you would have. You're the strongest person I know."

He brushed his thumb over her cheek, wiping away a stray tear. Emily's heart swelled, overflowing with love for this incredible man.

"I love you," she whispered.

Tom's smile widened. He leaned in, his breath warm against her lips.

"I love you too."

Their mouths met in a soft, lingering kiss. Emily melted into his arms, feeling truly at home for the first time in forever. With Tom by her side, she could conquer anything life threw their way. As long as they were together, that was all that mattered.

Cassidy let out a long, deep breath as she sank into the plush cushions of the living room sofa, the events of the past few weeks finally catching up with her. Though she was exhausted both mentally and physically from the chaos surrounding Morgan's murder, a sense of relief washed over her knowing that the real killer had been caught.

Justice had prevailed for Morgan. Jonathan would pay for his crimes, unable to hurt anyone else. And most importantly, her dad and Emily had cracked the case wide open with their tireless investigative work.

Cassidy smiled proudly, thinking of how fiercely the two of them had fought for the truth, never giving up even when all seemed lost. She was so grateful to have them both in her life. Not only were they an unstoppable crime-solving duo, but they'd also become like family to her over the years.

As if on cue, Tom emerged from the kitchen with two mugs of freshly brewed coffee in hand. He offered one to Cassidy before settling down in the armchair adjacent to her.

"How're you holding up, kiddo?" he asked gently.

Cassidy took a long sip, letting the rich aroma soothe her senses. "I'm okay. Tired, but...relieved. I can't thank you and Emily enough for everything you did."

Tom set down his mug and leaned forward, his eyes crinkling warmly. "You don't need to thank us, Cass. We'd do anything for you, you know that."

Cassidy nodded, emotion welling up in her chest. She knew how true that was. Her dad had always been her rock, her protector. And now Emily was part of that sacred circle too.

"I'm so proud of you both," Cassidy said thickly. "You make an amazing team."

Tom chuckled. "We do, don't we?" His expression grew serious again. "I'm just glad this is all over. Oakwood is safe again thanks to you and Emily."

Cassidy smiled, comforted by her father's quiet praise. With him and Emily watching over her, she knew everything would be okay.

Cassidy took a long sip of coffee, gathering her thoughts. She knew the relief was only temporary - there was still the matter of Clara and Charles' uncertain future.

"Dad," she began hesitantly. "What's going to happen to Clara and Charles now? With Ms. Reynolds...gone, they don't have a home here anymore."

Tom sighed deeply, the wrinkles on his forehead deepening. "I know. The situation isn't ideal. But we'll figure something out."

"Can't we do something?" Cassidy pleaded, setting her mug

down with an anxious clink. "They've been through so much already. It doesn't seem fair to uproot them again."

Tom looked thoughtful, his dark eyes distant. Cassidy could almost see the gears turning in his head.

"You really care about those kids, don't you?" he finally said.

Cassidy nodded emphatically. In the short time she'd known them, she'd grown incredibly fond of Clara and Charles. The thought of them having to leave Oakwood and start over tore at her heart.

Tom ran a hand through his salt-and-pepper hair. "Well, the house is plenty big enough..." he mused.

Cassidy perked up. "Wait, are you saying..."

"I can't make any promises yet," Tom said gently. "But let me talk to Emily. If anyone can figure something out, she can."

A swell of hope rose in Cassidy's chest. If her dad was on board with the idea, maybe there was a chance after all. She leapt up from the sofa and threw her arms around Tom.

"Thank you, Dad," she whispered, voice thick with emotion. "I know we can give them a good home here. You're the best."

Tom hugged her tightly, planting a kiss on the top of her head. "I'll do my best, kiddo. That's a promise."

Tom smiled as he watched his daughter hurry upstairs, her optimism infectious. He was still trying to wrap his head around the possibility of taking in three more kids, but Cassidy's big heart and Emily's formidable problem-solving skills might just make it work.

Speaking of Emily...Tom realized he hadn't seen her since they got home. The revelation about Jonathan had hit her hard; he could see it in her haunted eyes. She'd disappeared into the study almost immediately, needing time to process.

Tom headed down the hall and paused outside the study door. He could hear Emily inside, speaking in a low voice. Gently, he cracked the door open.

Emily stood with her back to him, silhouetted against the large bay window. One hand cradled her phone to her ear while the other rested lightly on her stomach. Tom felt a pang in his chest at how small and vulnerable she looked in that moment.

"I know, Mom," Emily was saying softly. "I just...I need some time. This wasn't easy for any of us."

She paused, listening, then sighed. "I promise I'll come visit soon. Just...not yet. I need to figure things out here first."

Another pause, then, "I know. I love you too. Kiss Dad for me."

Emily ended the call and leaned forward, resting her forehead against the cool glass. Tom took the opportunity to announce his presence.

"Rough day, huh?" he said gently.

Emily turned, looking weary but forcing a smile. "That's putting it mildly."

She crossed the room and sank onto the leather sofa, patting the spot beside her in invitation. Tom sat, taking her delicate hand in his.

They sat in pensive silence for a moment before Tom spoke again. "On a lighter note, Cassidy had an interesting idea earlier."

He explained his daughter's plea to take in Clara and Charles. Emily looked thoughtful as she listened.

"It would be a big change," Tom concluded. "Especially with the wedding coming up. What do you think?"

He studied Emily's face, wishing he could read her conflicted emotions. This would affect her new role as Cassidy's stepmom too.

Finally Emily smiled softly. "I think," she said, "that it sounds wonderful."

Tom blinked in surprise. "Really?"

"Of course!" Emily's eyes shone with affection. "You've always wanted a big family. And that house has enough room for an army. I'd love to give those kids a permanent home."

Tom pulled her into an embrace, relief washing over him. Only Emily truly understood his longing for family.

"Have I told you lately that you're amazing?" he murmured into her hair.

Emily laughed. "Flattery will get you everywhere, counselor."

They shared a tender kiss before Emily pulled back, her expression growing serious.

"There's something you should know first though," she said nervously. "Before we make any big decisions..."

Tom frowned. "What is it?"

Emily took a deep breath, meeting his gaze.

"I'm pregnant."

Tom's eyes went wide. For several heartbeats, he just stared at her wordlessly. Emily bit her lip.

"Tom? Say something, please."

A grin slowly spread across Tom's face. He whooped and pulled Emily into his arms again, spinning her around joyfully.

"This is incredible!" he exclaimed. "Emily, a baby! Our baby!"

Emily laughed, relief flooding through her.

Tom set her down gently, eyes shining. "Well, I'd say this settles it then. We've definitely got enough love for one more."

He caressed Emily's stomach tenderly.

"Our little family is growing," he whispered. "And I can't wait."

Emily smiled, placing her hand over Tom's. "Me too," she said softly. "But I have to admit, I'm a little nervous about handling three new kids plus a baby on the way."

She bit her lip uncertainly. "It's a big change. I know how much you want this, but I want to make sure we're really ready."

Tom nodded thoughtfully, his excitement dimming. "You're right, that's a lot to take on."

He considered for a moment. "Those kids have been through so much hardship already. They deserve stability and care. If we're not 100% confident we can provide that right now, we shouldn't rush into this."

Emily squeezed his hand gratefully. "I'm so glad you understand. But I must admit they are really cute. Maybe it's my hormones, but I really think i want this"

Tom pulled her close again. "Amazing Em! We'll figure this out together."

He smiled down at her belly. "Let's start on preparing for this little one first and we'll see what taking in those two entails"

Emily nodded, feeling relieved. As much as she wanted to help, she knew they had to be realistic.

Tom tilted her chin up gently. "You are an amazing woman, Emily, and I'm sure you'll be a fantastic mother."

Emily smiled up at him. "You're going to be an amazing dad."

They kissed once more, brimming with hope for the future ahead.

CHAPTER 19

The scent of freshly brewed coffee drifted from the kitchen as Emily flipped through wedding magazines at the dining room table. Tom entered with two mugs in hand, placing one in front of Emily before sitting down across from her.

"I still can't believe we're doing this," Emily said, eyes bright with excitement. "It feels like a dream."

Tom smiled, taking a sip of coffee. "Just think, in a few short months you'll officially be Mrs. Blackwell."

Emily's heart fluttered at the thought. "Have you given any more thought to venues?" she asked. "I was thinking somewhere outdoors could be nice."

"What about Willow Creek Vineyard?" Tom suggested. "We could have the ceremony in their garden under that big oak tree you love so much. The reception could spill out onto the vineyard - it would be beautiful."

Emily's mind filled with visions of exchanging vows surrounded by vines heavy with ripe grapes, fairy lights twinkling above the reception tables set along the rows. "That's perfect," she breathed.

Just then, Cassidy bounded into the kitchen, dropping her backpack on the floor before joining them at the table.

"Hey Dad, Emily, what's up?" she asked breezily, stealing a piece of bacon from the platter.

"We were just talking wedding venues," Tom replied. "How do you feel about having it at Willow Creek Vineyard?"

Cassidy's eyes lit up. "I love that idea! We could hang lanterns from the trees and have the florist put together wildflower arrangements for the tables. It's going to be magical."

Emily smiled at the girl's enthusiasm. "I'm so glad you're excited. We'd love your help with all the planning and prep."

"Just say the word!" Cassidy grabbed a stack of invitations. "Josh and I can start addressing these tonight and get them sent out."

Right on cue, the doorbell rang and Cassidy jumped up to answer it. Josh's smiling face appeared as he gave a little wave.

"Josh! Perfect timing," Cassidy said, pulling him inside. "We're getting started on the wedding plans."

Josh's eyes crinkled with warmth. "Anything you need, just let me know. I'm happy to help."

Tom watched the two huddle over the invitations, laughter spilling from their corner. He reached across the table and gave Emily's hand a squeeze, gratitude swelling in his chest for the family they were building together.

Emily squeezed Tom's hand in return, her green eyes meeting his with a joyful sparkle. "I'm so thankful for our little family," she said softly.

Just then, the front door swung open and two new faces appeared - Clara and Charles, their young foster children. Though they had only been with the Blackwells a short while, Emily and Tom had quickly grown to love them like their own.

"Clara, Charles, come on in," Tom beckoned warmly. "We're just going over plans for the wedding and could use some extra helpers."

Clara's dark eyes surveyed the scene, taking in the scattered invitations and floral samples. "It appears you have a monumental task ahead," she said wryly. "Perhaps Charles and I can lighten the burden."

Charles was already bouncing on his toes. "Yeah, put us to work! I wanna do something fun."

Cassidy waved them over. "You can help me and Josh with these invites. We'll make an assembly line."

The four huddled together, laughing and chatting as they folded and stuffed envelopes. Emily watched with satisfaction, then turned to Clara.

"I have a special project for you, if you're interested," she said. "I'd love for you to design some handmade decorations for the reception. You have such creative talent."

Clara looked touched. "I'd be honored. Just tell me your vision."

As they discussed flower arrangements and tablescapes, Tom put his arm around Emily. "Looks like our family is coming together perfectly," he said. "But I do have one more surprise up my sleeve."

He stood and cleared his throat. "Hey everyone, can we gather for a family meeting?"

Josh set down his stack of invitations and they all turned their attention to Tom. He smiled at each of them in turn.

"Emily and I have an announcement to make." He paused for dramatic effect. "We're expecting a new addition to the Blackwell family!"

Gasps and cheers erupted around the room. Cassidy leapt up to hug them both. "Oh my gosh, a baby! I'm going to be a big sister!"

Charles pumped his fist in the air. "This is awesome!"

One by one they offered hugs and congratulations, their faces glowing with joy. Tom wrapped an arm around Emily, both blinking back happy tears. This wedding was bringing them more than just a spouse - it was bringing them the family they'd always dreamed of.

Cassidy could hardly contain her excitement as she pulled Josh aside.

"I have amazing news too," she whispered. "We both got accepted to Harvard!"

Josh's eyes widened. "No way! We did it?"

Cassidy nodded, her smile stretching from ear to ear. She held up her acceptance letter.

Josh let out a whoop and picked her up in a hug, spinning her around. Their laughter drew the attention of the others.

"What's going on over there?" Tom asked.

"We got into Harvard!" Josh announced.

Another round of cheers went up. Charles grabbed Josh in a brotherly embrace. "That's awesome, man!"

Tom's voice grew thick with emotion. "I'm so proud of you both."

He pulled them in for a hug. Emily dabbed at her eyes with a tissue. "My kids are off to Harvard," she marveled.

"We should celebrate," Clara declared. "Let's have a family game night!"

"Great idea," Tom said. "I'll order some pizzas."

Soon they were gathered in the living room, bellies full of pizza, playing an intense round of Pictionary. Laughter echoed off the walls as they tried to guess each other's drawing skills.

Charles groaned as Cassidy easily guessed his rendition of a firetruck. "How are you so good at this?"

"Years of practice beating Dad," she grinned.

Tom feigned offense. "Just wait until Charades is up next."

The hours flew by, filled with teasing banter and good-natured competition. For a while, the looming changes ahead faded into the background. In this moment, they were just a family, relishing their time together.

Tom glanced at his watch and stood up from the couch. "It's getting late. I should start cleaning up."

Emily touched his arm. "Leave it for now. I wanted to talk to you about something."

She turned to the kids. "Would you give us a few minutes?"

Cassidy and Josh exchanged a knowing look as they herded Charles and Clara upstairs.

Tom raised an eyebrow. "What's going on?"

Emily took a deep breath. "With the kids leaving soon, it got me thinking about the future. And I realized something." She met his eyes. "I want Clara and Charles to be a permanent part of this family."

Tom's face lit up. "You mean officially adopting them?"

She nodded. "Only if you want that too. I know it's a big commitment, but they deserve stability. And I can't imagine this family without them now."

"Neither can I." Tom took her hands in his. "Let's give them the home they've always deserved."

Emily threw her arms around him, emotion welling up. "Thank you, Tom."

He held her close, savoring the moment. Then he pulled back, a playful glint in his eyes. "Should we tell the kids now or let them sweat it out a bit?"

Emily laughed. "I think they've waited long enough."

She called upstairs, "Clara, Charles, can you come back down here?"

The patter of footsteps preceded their arrival. Charles bounced down the stairs two at a time. "What's up?"

Tom smiled at them warmly. "Emily and I have something we'd like to ask you."

Clara's eyes widened, immediately grasping the implication. Charles looked between them quizzically.

"We were hoping," Emily began, "that you would allow us to adopt you. To make you permanent members of the Blackwell family."

"Really?" Charles burst out. Clara just stared, stunned into silence.

"Really," Tom confirmed. "If you'll have us."

Charles whooped and leapt into Tom's arms. Clara walked over more slowly, still processing it all.

"You would do that for us?" she finally asked in a hushed voice.

Emily wrapped her in a fierce hug. "In a heartbeat."

Overwhelmed, Clara finally relaxed into her embrace. The promise of family, once lost, now found again.

Tom took a deep breath, surveying the scene before him. The vineyard was a flurry of activity as the Blackwell family and their friends put the finishing touches on the wedding venue.

Cassidy weaved through the rows of vines, hanging strands of lights that cast a warm glow as the sun began its descent. Emily directed Josh and Charles on the placement of chairs, ensuring each row was perfectly spaced. Clara carefully arranged the floral centerpieces on the tables, taking a step back occasionally to admire her work.

Tom felt a presence by his side. Nora appeared, two glasses of wine in hand. "Here. You look like you could use this."

Tom accepted it gratefully. "I can't believe this day is finally here. Part of me worries something will go wrong."

Nora clasped his shoulder reassuringly. "The only thing going wrong today is you driving yourself crazy. Everything is perfect."

Tom smiled, allowing her confidence to temper his nerves. His gaze found Emily across the vineyard, radiant in her wedding dress as she embraced Cassidy.

"You're right. As long as they're here, that's all that matters."

Nora patted his back. "Now go get ready. I'll keep overseeing things here."

Tom headed off, weaving through the vines towards the small cottage serving as their dressing area. Donning his tuxedo, he took a moment alone to collect himself.

This was it. The moment he would pledge himself to Emily in front of those dearest to them. Not just a union, but a new family. A second chance he never imagined possible.

Ready, Tom stepped outside, where Charles waited to escort him down the aisle. "You look sharp, Dad," he grinned.

Hearing those words, Tom had to blink back tears. "Thank you, son."

Charles' smile grew wider. Together, they made their way to the ceremony site.

Guests were seated and a hush fell over the vineyard. Then the strings of Pachelbel's Canon in D began, and all eyes turned expectantly down the aisle.

Emily appeared on the arm of Josh, a vision in lace and tulle. Tom's breath caught at the sight of her, more beautiful than he could've dreamed.

Reaching the altar, Emily and Tom joined hands, lost in each other's gaze. The officiant began speaking, but Tom heard only the pounding of his own heart.

This was really happening. The woman before him, his soulmate, was pledging herself to him for life.

When prompted for vows, Tom recited his with conviction: "Emily, you are the missing piece of my heart. Our path here wasn't easy, but I would walk it a thousand times if it led me back to you. I promise to spend every day proving worthy of your love."

Emily's eyes glistened as she responded in kind. Then finally, it was time.

"I now pronounce you husband and wife. You may kiss the bride!"

As their lips met, cheers erupted across the vineyard. Tom held Emily close, acutely aware of the preciousness of this moment. A new chapter was beginning.

❋ ❋ ❋

The warm autumn sun streamed through the crimson leaves as Cassidy and Josh strolled hand-in-hand across Harvard Yard. This historic place that had lived so vividly in their dreams was now their reality.

Cassidy breathed it all in—the imposing brick buildings, the crowds of students hurrying to class, the energy and excitement palpable in the air. After years of hard work, they had finally arrived.

Stopping beneath the stately elm trees, Cassidy turned to Josh, eyes shining. "Can you believe we actually made it here? All the late nights studying, all the college apps...it was all worth it for this moment."

Josh pulled her close. "I know. If you told me a year ago that we'd be standing here together, I wouldn't have believed it."

He gently brushed a strand of hair from her face. "But we did make it. And now a whole new adventure begins."

Cassidy nodded, a mix of exhilaration and nervousness welling up inside. She knew the road ahead would be challenging, but with Josh by her side, she was ready for whatever came next.

As students milled around them, the bells of a nearby chapel began to chime. Cassidy closed her eyes and made a wish—that this place would be everything they hoped for, that their dreams would come true.

When she opened them, Josh was gazing at her softly. No words were needed. They both knew this was only the beginning. Leaning in, their lips met in a kiss brimming with promise.

The chimes faded, but Cassidy and Josh remained locked in a tender embrace—two kindred spirits ready to take on the future together.

CHAPTER 20

Tom paused in the doorway, a content smile spreading across his rugged face. Morning sunlight filtered into the cozy kitchen, bathing his daughter Cassidy and her friend Josh in its warm glow as they sat at the round wooden table. The rich aroma of brewed coffee mingled with the mouthwatering scent of sizzling bacon coming from the stovetop where Emily stood over a hissing skillet.

"Morning, you two," Tom said, folding his arms across his broad chest as he leaned against the door frame.

Cassidy's blue eyes danced with mischief as she grinned up at her father. "Morning, Dad. I hope you're hungry, Mom's going all out this morning."

"I'm always hungry for your mom's cooking," Tom chuckled. His heart swelled at the scene of domestic bliss - his little girl on the cusp of adulthood, still finding joy in teasing her old man.

Josh let out an exaggerated groan, clutching his stomach. "Ugh, stop talking about food, I'm starving over here!"

Cassidy playfully swatted Josh's shoulder. "So dramatic! Here, have some more coffee while we wait." She topped off Josh's mug from the pot on the table, then leaned back in her chair.

"Thanks," Josh said, flashing a dimpled grin. "So, as I was saying before we were rudely interrupted by the old man over there..."

Cassidy burst into giggles. "Old man? Real nice, Josh."

Tom couldn't help but chuckle as he watched the two banter back and forth, their laughter filling the cozy kitchen. It amazed him to see the young man Josh had become after the tragedy he had endured - still quick to laugh, still finding light even in darkness. Cassidy had been a lifeline for him this past year, her humor and loyalty pulling him through. And now, Tom sensed a new closeness between them, a budding affection.

Pride swelled in Tom's chest again. No matter what storms raged outside these walls, within them, there was joy. There was family. There was love.

Tom's gaze drifted to the window, where he could see Nora across the street, bustling about inside her diner. Even from a distance, her warmth was palpable. As she flitted between tables chatting with customers, her smile lit up the space around her.

Nora had an uncanny ability to make everyone feel at home. Her diner was the heartbeat of their little town, drawing in folks from all walks of life. To many, she was the mother they never had - always ready with a listening ear or words of wisdom.

Tom thought back to when he had first returned to Oakwood, broken and adrift after tragedy struck. Nora had taken one look at his hollow eyes and immediately wrapped him in a hug. "Welcome home, Tommy," she had said. "We'll get through this together."

And they had. Nora was there for all the ups and downs since - late-night talks when grief overwhelmed him, proud cheers at Cassidy's ballet recitals, celebrations of life's little victories. She was family.

As Tom watched Nora now, he felt a swell of gratitude. So much had changed from a year ago, when Oakwood was shrouded in suspicion and fear after the murder. But Nora had remained a beacon of light through it all. Her love and resilience had helped guide them forward, out of darkness and into hope.

Later they crossed the street to go see Nora, Cassidy's laughter rang out, her voice a welcome melody amidst the diner's familiar clatter. She was perched on a stool at the counter, eyes alight with mirth as she traded quips with Josh. He sat beside her, grinning as he shook his head in amusement.

"You're incorrigible, you know that?" Josh said, giving her shoulder a playful nudge.

Cassidy's smile turned impish. "Oh please, you love it."

She had a vibrancy to her today that warmed Tom's heart. The weight that had pressed down on his daughter after her mother's death had finally begun to lift this past year. He knew the journey wasn't over, but Cassidy was thriving - coming fully into her own.

Tom watched as Josh looped an affectionate arm around her, his eyes brimming with admiration. They had forged an unbreakable bond through shared hardship. Josh had proven himself a loyal friend when Cassidy needed one most. He was family now too.

Cassidy leaned into Josh, her expression softening. "Really though, thank you for always having my back," she said.

"Of course," Josh replied. "I'm so proud of you, Cass. You amaze me every day."

She smiled, tilting her head up to plant a quick kiss on his cheek. They stayed like that for a moment, two kindred souls finding solace in each other.

Tom's heart swelled. The future was uncertain, but he knew his daughter had found something real. As long as she and Josh had each other, they would be okay.

Tom cleared his throat, catching their attention.

"Oh, hey Dad!" Cassidy said, turning to face him with a sheepish grin.

Tom smiled, though he kept his tone serious. "You know I trust you both, but don't stay out too late tonight."

"We won't Mr. Blackwell," Josh assured.

Cassidy rolled her eyes playfully. "You worry too much."

"It's a dad's job to worry," Tom replied. His protective instincts had grown sharper since Emily came into their lives. He wanted to shelter Cassidy from further heartbreak.

Just then, the screen door creaked open and Nora emerged carrying a tray of lemonade. Her presence seemed to cast a spell of calm over the porch.

"Now Tom, you have to let our girl spread her wings," she chided gently.

Tom sighed, knowing Nora spoke the truth. Cassidy needed freedom to chart her own course. With Emily and Nora's guidance, he could allow it.

"You're right," Tom conceded. He turned back to Cassidy and Josh. "Just stay safe and have fun tonight."

Cassidy beamed, throwing her arms around him in a quick hug. "Thanks Dad!"

As the two young adults hurried off, Nora handed Tom a glass of lemonade.

"Change is never easy," she said sagely. "But you've raised a strong young woman. She'll do great things."

Tom nodded, comforted by her reassuring wisdom. With Nora's

help, they would navigate this new chapter together.

Tom's gaze followed Cassidy and Josh as they strolled hand-in-hand towards town, their laughter fading into the distance. He envied their carefree innocence.

Turning to Nora, he said "I don't know how we'd manage without you keeping us on track."

She waved her hand dismissively. "Oh Tom, you give me too much credit."

"No, I mean it," Tom insisted. "You've been a rock for this family, for me..." His voice grew thick with emotion.

Nora had lost so much, yet still gave endlessly to others. She was the heart of their community - welcoming strangers like family, listening without judgement, and nourishing broken spirits.

Tom realized he'd taken her stalwart presence for granted. But seeing Cassidy blossom under her care awoke a deep sense of gratitude in him.

"We're so lucky to have you, Nora," he said, his eyes glistening. "I don't think I've ever properly thanked you for everything you do."

Nora tutted, but seemed touched. She gave his hand a maternal squeeze.

"It's nothing, love. Just knowing I can make a difference is thanks enough." Her humble nature never ceased to amaze Tom.

He pulled her into a fierce hug. One thing was certain - he would never let Nora feel unappreciated again. She was the keystone their family, and Oakwood itself, was built upon.

* * *

Tom leaned against the porch railing, gazing out at the expanse of golden shoreline as the sun dipped below the horizon. The faint laughter of children playing along the beach drifted on the salty breeze. He took a deep breath, drinking in the familiar seaside air.

A rare sense of peace settled over him. For the first time in years, the future seemed bright. Free from the darkness of the past, his family now had a chance to heal and thrive.

Tom's joy was palpable as he envisioned lazy weekends filled with beach picnics, bike rides along the coast, and cozy movie nights piled on the couch. The coming days would be rich with love and laughter, binding them all closer together.

The screen door creaked open and Cassidy, Emily who is now slowly showing, Clara and Charles stepped out to join him.

Cassidy buried her face in her dad's shoulder, tears of joy dampening his shirt. She had imagined this moment countless times, but now that Harvard was real, the emotions overwhelmed her.

"I can't believe I'm actually going," she said, her voice muffled.

Tom stroked her hair. "You've worked so hard for this. You deserve it, plus can you imagine Christmas break all 6 and half of us." They shared a laugh

He thought back to all the late nights helping her study, the weekends spent editing application essays. Every sacrifice had been worth it to see her follow her dreams, and in the end have his own come true.

BOOKS IN THIS SERIES

Blackwell

Death Of A Fisherman

Such A Pta

Won't Stop Believin

Till Death Do We Start

www.ingramcontent.com/pod-product-compliance
Lightning Source LLC
Chambersburg PA
CBHW070847280626
47161CB00017B/2915